LEMON TARTS IN SPACE!

Cameron Fucile

For Sam

Thank you for always believing in my
stupidity

TABLE OF CONTENTS

CHAPTER ONE: <u>The Clunker</u>

The Clunker was floating in open space. This was not ideal. Spaceships are traditionally outfitted with boosters and thrusters and all sorts of big, scary engines that help them drive the wrong way up into the sky and stay afloat once they get there — but sometimes, things break.

Even the fanciest gadgets, the satellite dishes, the wings, they're all just one screw-up away from being paperweights. *The Clunker* was one such monument to user error, and we join the ship as it hovers, motionless, somewhere between Jupiter and the one with the rings.

"This is the Captain speaking, again. If the first mate could report to — uh — just call me back. Please. I think something bad has happened." He switched off the intercom and continued, to himself. "They're still mad, that's fine. I can see things from their perspective, I've said that all along."

He tried to rally, but just couldn't let it go. "Those things are wrong *all the time!* Leadership is strong direction, instinct, and no blinking red light is going to tell me how to captain my — "

He trailed off with a long, wistful sigh. While I'm here, I feel the need to clarify that he's talking about the 'blinking red light' on the *fuel gauge*.

"Still, it's been a week now, since we ran out of gas and they locked me in the" — he cleared his throat — "cockpit. Tempers are running hot."

Mutiny had been the only real option for the crew of *The Clunker*. Captain Duncan Arugula was a strong leader, no question. He could rally his crew with a well-timed speech from the flight deck. He could pace with purpose and bravado, delivering important decisions with eyebrows that were somehow both tented and furrowed at the exact same time. There was a stroke of real heroism to Duncan Arugula. The problem was that he was also just slightly stupid.

"A plan, that's all I need. You win 'em back, *dazzle 'em,* that's the only thing that matters. No grudges, no retribution, just *a plan.*" He started pacing, trying to find his rhythm. "The radar, the engine, the exhaust pipes — the mud flaps on the wings, if we" — another grumble — "waggle them up and down fast enough, like flippers!"

He raised his hands in mock surrender. "Yes, it would take a while — *have to prepare for their objections* — but eventually we'd shuffle straight back into Jupiter's orbit, and then it's all gravy!" He realized that his hands had moved to his hips and smiled approvingly. "We just flap the wings. Maybe move some cabinets, trash cans to the front of the ship. Make it top heavy." His smile widened. "Like a bird with a big 'ole head. A pelican! *Operation Pelican*. We just flap to safety."

He snapped and started pacing again. "There's another plan, right there. Ten seconds of work. *We're gonna be fine!*"

The first few days after Captain Arugula's detainment had been very productive. Tranquil. The flight crew radioed for help and everyone else took up a sudden interest in alternative fuel sources. No idea was too outlandish. No possibility was too remote. The kitchen staff went straight to the root of the problem — the smell. Gasoline is a dreadful sludge, and what does it even do, *really?* Smells acidic and burns easy. And so they proposed that the engines be filled instead with lemon juice and matches, which would presumably work just as well.

The navigator got even more creative, suggesting that they hang butterfly nets out the windows to catch passing asteroids and meteors, which could then be shoveled into the cold, dormant engines — and I quote — *just like we used to do with choo choo trains*. Oh, and for their part, the flight crew just kept on sending out distress calls, although, regrettably, these impassioned pleas were being broadcast over the *intercom*, not the radio. Captain Duncan Arugula was not the only idiot aboard *The Clunker,* and they were not going to be fine.

"To my loyal and noble crew — this is your Captain. I have decided that our present setback is nothing to be worried about. In fact, I think we should take a break from all this worrying and celebrate, together." His contented sigh was a wall of fuzz over the intercom. "In my office, top drawer of my desk, you will find a wonderful recipe for lemon tart. Old family recipe, the perfect thing to help us all — unwind. My father used to make us one every Sunday."

He caught himself and refocused. "Anyway, when the tart is in the oven, why doesn't someone come and — unlock the door. I'd love to see everyone again, catch up. And if you do want to talk business, I have a few ideas about how we could — "

He kept talking, but — ya know — try to imagine him slowly fading into the background as our narrative interest wanes.

A grim suspicion might be creeping into your mind, as you ponder this bunch of dummies stuck in outer space. Why isn't the crew answering their beleaguered Captain? Why would a spaceship have an oven? Both fair questions. If you picture *The Clunker* once more — just hanging there, suspended in boundless nothing — focus in on all those engines and thrusters we discussed earlier. Now, there certainly isn't *fuel* in any of them anymore. No fire or sparkiness left. The lemon juice and matches have all floated away. But if you zoom in closer, and imagine yourself to be both very small and very devious, those exhaust pipes might start to look a lot like *open doorways.*

"—and if that doesn't work, I know some of the cabinets are bolted down — might be hard to move — we *could* look into building some escape pods. I know we probably should have talked about those *a while ago,* but it always felt — somehow — insulting. I didn't want the flight crew to think they were replaceable. And you know, between figuring out the seating arrangements, the extra fuel, all the upholstery work — it just seemed like an unnecessary hassle!"

He froze as the crushing guilt washed over him. "But, here we are. I don't know. We don't have to talk about that right now. Dessert and hugs all around — a happy reunion awaits!

'Monster' is a very loaded term, and 'alien' is a little played out, so let's just call it a problem. The 'Problem' had snuck aboard four days into the Captain's quarantine. He was small and round, about the size of a lemon tart. The Problem had two eyes, more teeth than I would prefer, and an insatiable, unending, unimaginable *appetite*. The creature came from a far-off planet with an unpronounceable name and a somewhat simplistic economy. When these Problems were hungry, they attacked and devoured anything they could find. Then they slept for a while, woke up, yawned horribly, and the whole cycle started again.

"The engineers really wouldn't be needed in an escape pod. *What is there to engineer?* No navigation system" — he snorted — "no *kitchen* either, come to think of it. Guess they can stay behind too. But hey, someone has to stay with the ship, keep an eye on things." He caught his own reflection in the cockpit windshield and hurriedly continued. "We'll come back for them. *I* will come back for them. A Captain never abandons his ship, but he might

— *have to* — sneak out for a bit, occasionally, to get some help."

A few of these globular green Problems had grown to enormous size. The more they ate, the stronger they became, and the bigger their next meal could be. If you have a telescope at hand, point it towards the sun, tilt it a bit to the left, then a bit more — just swing it around for a while. When you've calmed down, look for Jupiter — the big blue gassy one towards the back. You can focus and readjust, twiddle all the knobs you want. It's not there. No, in its place is a titanic green *Problem* with two eyes and lots of teeth.

A furious, panting snarl echoed through *The Clunker* as the Problem raced through its pipes and hallways. Hideous burbles and snarls caught on the sleek, secondhand paneling, instantly rusting any exposed screws. This particular Problem was the ambitious middle son of the blob that ate Jupiter. He has grown somewhat *thicker* since he came aboard, but no less voracious.

After he ate the crew, the Problem had napped a while in the engine room. When he awoke, and yawned horribly, he had almost left the ship. Only two things had stopped him. The first was his enhanced bulk, which made the exhaust pipes suddenly unfeasible. He'd wobbled around for a while looking for a nice side door or open window, but something had interrupted his search. This something was the second something which changed his mind and prolonged his time aboard *The Clunker.* The Captain's emphatic, uncertain ramblings over the intercom sparked the Problem's interest, but he knew from previous hijackings that computer voices were not always edible.

The Problem closed both of his eyes and sniffed deeply. This was followed by a truly despicable, shockingly *wet* cackle, and then another round of excited snort burbles.

Yeah, let's call that a positive I.D. on Captain Duncan Arugula. And there he goes, tearing through the ship looking for its final inhabitant, while he digests the rest of the crew. The Captain, for his part, was still quite busy reminiscing over the intercom. I think he's still going on about that lemon tart.

"It was an anniversary of some sort. Might have been my birthday. A most welcome surprise. I love surprises." He gasped, and there was a smile in his voice. "Maybe that's what this is! Oh, you guys are the worst. Very sneaky. Here, why don't I close my eyes? I'll even turn around and face the wall. *No peeking!* Ha. I must have lost track of time in here.

When I open my eyes, you'd better not all be in here with a fresh lemon tart!"

The Problem had grown *excited* when he smelled the crew all gathered together in the mess hall. A few members of the kitchen staff had almost been swallowed whole. The Problem tried not to do this often, of course. It gave him a headache, and the acid that made up his body — and personality — took a while to dissolve large, dense meals. Most of the engineers had been eaten more respectfully — one gnashing, horrifying bite at a time. Indigestion could be a problem for Problems, even if portion control and table manners were not.

You know, judging by their hunting patterns and limitless growth, I can only conclude that Problems do not poop. I suppose the acid just breaks it all down and repurposes the goo. Very efficient for space travel, really. Environmentally friendly. Still, it is *unnerving* to see the First Mate's head suspended in a homicidal jelly mold.

"I think I hear footsteps! This really is the best birthday ever. You *totally* got me. Totally. I was actually getting kind of scared in here. Great prank though, good job everybody. What else do you have planned? Maybe we *do* have fuel and we're not stuck out here after all. *Very thorough!"* A manic laugh shot out over the intercom. "I thought we were all gonna die!"

The Problem thudded hard against the door of the cockpit.

"I can't open the door, guys. *You locked me in, remember?"*

Another thud, and then an excited little snarl.

"Everything okay out there? I hope you used a potholder to carry the tart." He could feel the hope slipping away, but persevered. "Wouldn't want you to burn yourselves." Those faint, ugly noises were all in his head — they had to be. "Can I open my eyes yet? Yeah, I think I'm just gonna — it's still a great surprise, but in case you need help with anythi-*ah!"*

The noise that escaped him was unbecoming of a Captain. It was a scream of surprise and understandable disgust, but the whole thing was delivered at an *uninspiring* pitch. His voice remained stuck in a wilting falsetto. "*What* is that? Oh God, it looks so mad. Look at those teeth! And why is it *green?* Is that a bad sign?" He slowed his breathing and adopted an unconvincing authoritative tone. "Okay — come on. Rally, Captain. People are relying on you, you can't go all — *oh no.* The crew. *The crew."*

He switched to a mutter, as though there was anyone left alive to hear him. "Not one of my better birthdays then, no it is not! Alright, let's assume the crew is … hiding. Evasive maneuvers." He was starting to hyperventilate again, whispering furiously. "They are absolutely dead. Every single one of them. *Look at those teeth!*"

He made another valiant attempt at normalcy. "Stop it, Duncan. Everything is under control. That door is strong, looks like some kind of metal. This ship is built like a tank. An old tank, *a classic!* Everything's fine. You're fine. You just need a plan — right now."

Metal is stronger than wood. Heavier too, but a *wooden* spaceship might struggle during takeoff. The entirety of *The Clunker* was made out of metal. Some of it was rusted and most of it was cheap, but it *was* metal. The engineers had deemed the door to the cockpit particularly important when they were drawing up the initial blueprints for the ship. No expense had been spared — I assume. It all just looks sort of grey now, but there are lots of sturdy bolts and screws in the door. *I* couldn't break it down, and I doubt you could either.

But *we* are not made of acid. The Problem was already melting through the door and scratching at it with those pointy little pumpkin teeth. Captain Arugula had about ten seconds left to think up an ingenious plan.

"Help! Oh I don't wanna die! *Help!*" He blinked, for what felt like the first time in a while. "That's — all I really have to say, I guess. Don't need this anymore." The intercom went dead as he dropped the receiver. "Really wish I'd installed a few escape pods. I just — I crunched the numbers, thought about it, and decided *aliens probably weren't real!* Or if they *were*, they'd be nice. Most people are nice, right?"

The cockpit door had started to hiss, and the unholy sounds of the Problem were getting louder. They both knew what was happening, and it was happening quickly.

"Gross! *Ah!*"

He kicked it. All that time to plan and strategize and the intrepid Captain *kicked* the Problem. His boot is going to melt away to nothing. Might even lose a big toe! He broke into an uneven run, and it looked like he was crying a bit too, but that might have been the aftershock of the pastry letdown. What a fool.

The Problem seemed less than thrilled with the interaction as well, snarling and twitching, climbing up the walls. His breathing slowed to a stuttered whine, barely even a pant, and then the nodding very suddenly stopped. And like a wolf howling at the moon, the Problem unleashed a feral, teeth-shattering squeal.

Here we go. I was expecting another sniff, something to help locate the scurrying Captain, but the Problem's rage appears to have overwhelmed his reason. Must be embarrassing, I suppose. His father ate a planet and here's some bakery-obsessed incompetent playing kickball with his forehead.

"Good luck finding me, *you rancid blob!*" The Captain was back on the intercom, and I'd be willing to bet there were still tears in his eyes. But the sudden bravado, the machismo — he was overshooting the mark. "I know this ship better than anyone. Oh, and don't even *think* about running away. I've locked every door and window, and activated a *high-end* security system. Who knows, maybe I even turned on the" — his voice cracked — "heat-seeking missile defense laser beams! The lava floors! The garbage disposal!"

He ran out of breath at *exactly* the wrong time, and stumbled over the punchline with a pathetic wheeze. "*Any step you take in any direction could be your doom!*"

The Problem did not speak English. To be fair, there had never been much use for language during his upbringing. His education didn't extend far beyond 'don't eat your brothers' and his father's approval or disapproval was easily communicated through grunts. The Captain's threats and bluffs were of no interest to the Problem. He was still a little hungry after the crew, and there was still one more snack available. Besides, it was a long trip home and he needed to look strong and grown-up at the next family reunion.

Duncan was working as fast as his trembling hands could manage. The fear was really starting to get to him. He thought he could feel an organ shutting down. Maybe it was a spleen? Hard to tell. He was whispering to himself, trying to drown out the slurping cacophony of the approaching Problem. "He should be nice and scared now. Yessir. *Rattled.* And more importantly, I have control of my ship again." He swallowed hard.

"The crew — was not hiding. Some pretty awful residue back there. Just me now. Just the Captain, going down with his ship." He clenched his jaw shut to keep his teeth from chattering. "I have no choice. I adore *The Clunker*, more than anything else in the whole universe, but I have no choice."

He punched in one last command and a dry electronic voice rang out through across the flight deck. "*INITIATE. SELF-DESTRUCT. ONE MINUTE.*"

The Captain didn't even stop for a quick salute. Every last second mattered. "Gotta hide now. Might taunt him again, if I have time, to throw him off the scent — but not here. Too exposed, too predictable." He cocked his head to the side. "Why am I talking to myself? Oh, right — because everyone else was eaten! Alright. Might as well keep it going. Forty-five seconds now. Let's go, Captain."

I guess he did have a plan. It's not a great one, but he probably won't lose the other foot — until the spaceship explodes. I find myself feeling wistful, as we stare down mechanical annihilation in the middle of this endless black abyss. *Maybe that was grumpier than it was wistful.*

The Problem — monster, alien, blob, creature, *whatever* — was slamming open doors and sniffing at air vents. It even found the mainframe controls and the master computer that the Captain had used to activate the self-destruct, but it was too late. All the electrodes or little vibrating strings — whatever makes computers work — they had already set the detonation in motion. Explosive devices were heating up, hard drives were spinning furiously, and all the engines were roaring on empty stomachs.

The Problem phlegm-sniffed a whole hot air balloon's worth of air in one big swig. His brain blazed through the influx of data, until he ripped a wretched, splattering burp that might have been meant as a gasp. The Problem devolved into excited, crunchy murmurings. He had the scent again, and — *ugh* — the First Mate's head was just a skull now. Must be making room for the next course.

Just look at him move. The Problem didn't take corners so much as he headbutted a wall and shrapneled in a new direction. He was sweating acid now. The floor melted away beneath him, revealing all sorts of important-looking cables. The Problem was heading back to the center of the ship, past the residue of the late crew. He was a born hunter, an unholy cross between a bloodhound and a gummy bear.

The Captain hadn't left any footprints to track — a compliment to his hygiene, to be sure — but there was an aroma. High stress situation, it's probably been a while since he applied deodorant. I'm not saying he's a bad guy, but it made him easier to track.

"Come on, come on. This *should* work." His voice echoed against the metal, even in a husky whisper. "It's a premium unit, the *one* thing

we splurged on. This is a good plan, *to live* —
not a bad way to die. You are Captain Duncan
Arugula and — "

He sniffed and recoiled, banging his head
on the cramped walls. "What is that smell? Is
that me? Woof."

As the computer's merciless countdown
entered single digits, the Problem crashed into
the kitchen and made a strange barking noise.
There was a desperation to it, like the
creature knew something bad was about to
happen.

He banged the door of the refrigerator
open and closed, melted the cabinets apart, and
paused briefly in front of the oven to spit out
the First Mate's jawbone. The bone clattered
on some hurriedly removed oven racks as the
Problem and the Captain made eye contact
through the glass of the oven door.

"Well, yeah. I mean, that is clearly not
a lemon tart."

The Clunker self-destructed in a
sparkling, majestic blaze. The engines exploded
and the computers sizzled. Bursts of fire and
electricity lit up the night and crackled out
across the blank canvas of the universe. Cheap,
rusty metal collapsed and twisted into
nothingness. The crew was somewhat hurriedly
cremated. The Problem was vaporized in the

initial blast, all but one angry little green eye that was plastered to the oven door. And the Captain, Captain Duncan Arugula, was left singed but alive inside the reinforced, luxury space oven that was now soaring at an incredibly high speed back towards Jupiter. Or — towards the murderous green blob that had *taken the place* of Jupiter.

A thought struck the Captain then, but it was the wrong thought. A slightly stupid thought that undermined his heroism and ingenuity even in this shining moment.

"Maybe it was lime."

Chapter Two: <u>Electric Tumor</u>

Space travel — I mean, where do I even start? Not one of humanity's better ideas. Consider the much-discussed Apollo program. Took 'em eleven at-bats to — oh, that's right — slingshot *around* the moon? Anyone can do that, it's just gravitational pull. You wanna see something impressive? I can make a yoyo go real fast, make a dead stop, hover in place, and then shoot right back up to where it started. Even better, I can do it all day long, for a buck fifty. No rocket fuel, no marshmallow suits with a toilet built in, no trillion dollar expense for the taxpayer.

It's an embarrassment, really, publicly failing at something eleven times on the world stage. And then, when we did *eventually* get there, what did we find? The cure for cancer? The meaning of life? Oil? No. We found rocks, and I don't know about you — maybe I'm totally wrong about this — but in my extensive travels, I've seen forests and beaches and mountains and hills and parking garages and you know what there never seems to be a shortage of? You know what I can't seem to stop pulling out of my shoes and tripping over? *Rocks.*

Pebbles, boulders, everything in between — we've got so many extra, unneeded, superfluous rocks that children keep them as pets. And the crown jewel, that big dumb grey yoyo in the sky, is our ultimate prize. The largest and most useless rock in our formidable collection — the moon.

Was it all worth it? Who's to say — *unless* there was more to the story. Unless there was some other reason, some hidden, clandestine motive behind our endless, expensive mission. Unless — the Apollo program wasn't about 'the moon' at all.

As you might imagine, it all started with Apollo One — and the Russians. It was an age of paranoia, pastel colors, wood paneling, the Cold War — or was that later? It all runs together. The space race, they called it, a gold rush for scientific advancement and international espionage. America's brightest minds all working together to achieve something that people just keep telling me is important, somehow. Apollo One was the culmination of their efforts, can't have gone that well though. Probably top heavy with fuel, or flew in circles. Back to the drawing board.

Apollo Two: gotta bring in the big guns, maybe some of those rehabbed Nazi scientists we keep in the back. But alas, that one didn't work either. Let's say it blew up on the launch pad, that had to happen at some point. Lucky number three, the hat trick, that one came next. Hadn't gotten the suits quite right, so the guys were liquified on takeoff. Apollo Four was a complete reboot, they just sent a passenger jet up up and away. Might've worked too, if it hadn't been for the Bermuda Triangle. Swallowed it right up, burped in our faces and asked for seconds.

Apollo Five didn't fare much better, even though it was built completely out of aluminum foil. Aerodynamic, sleek, light as a feather, but not — as it turns out — as insulated as one might hope. Looked like Pompeii. That one cost them in the morale department. Hard to recruit for Apollo *Six* after jiffy popping an entire crew. And by the time they hit double digits, we were really scraping the bottom of the barrel. Russia was laughing in our face, public support was turning against the whole idea of wasting money, and something had to change, *fast*.

The breathless public gathered around their rickety old rabbit ear televisions as a haggard newsman slid into frame and reshuffled his papers, trying to avoid eye contact with the camera. "Fresh off the presses, reporting in from Washington D.C., we can officially confirm reports that the recently launched

Apollo 10 rocket has touched down at the bottom of the ocean."

He arched his eyebrows and leaned back, carefully avoiding any recognizable human emotion. "A NASA spokesperson, when asked for comment, categorically refused to confirm the rumor that they had placed the rocket in the launcher upside down. Meanwhile, the Dirty Red Communist Devils have succeeded in launching yet another miniature schnauzer into the sun. *More at eleven.*"

Desperation takes many forms, but it always smells the same. The space travel program had about forty-eight hours left before it completely ran out of money, and suddenly, there were *no* bad ideas. Unfortunately, there were almost exclusively *bad* scientists left to act on those almost universally atrocious ideas, and well — you might be able to see where this is going. Lotta dummies, lotta money, very little time.

These were not the names you know, not the heroes and pioneers you learned about in school. These were the other ones, the last in their class who were still technically recruited to serve the Cold War effort. The scraps, the dullards, the dolts — this was their moment to shine.

"What if — and hear me out on this — *what if* we just built a" — the scientist tapped a pen against the desk, working through incalculable, impossible theorems — "like out of the material that we're using for the outside of the rockets, what if we just used that and built, like, a suit of armor out of it? Stuck one guy in there, he knows where to go, he can just look at the moon, maybe give him flippers to wear so he can steer better. No computers, no launchers — huh. No fuel. Nowhere to put the" — his pen stopped dead. "Alright, never mind, but what *if* — "

You know, that sounded like an anecdote, some sick joke whipped up by someone who is totally ignorant of scientific history, but it's not. There's an official transcript. A paper trail. He tried to expense the flippers. Oh yes, our best and brightest rallied behind their dummy king and tried it. There was some heated disagreement, allegedly, over whether they should use rocket boots for propulsion or just have him hold on tight to a big firework, and in the end — well, it didn't really get that far.

The police report called it an electrical fire, but in practice it was closer to a nuclear meltdown. Those labs are full of all sorts of flammable, explosive, toxic, and experimental doodads — and you'd better believe they *all* exploded when the astronaut tried to light up a cigarette.

"Where am I? Oh god, what happened? Was it the Reds?" The astronaut — well, really he was more of a test pilot — and not even that. He'd come in the day before to interview for a technician job. His resume cites a long career as a 'mecha-dynamic electrical activation engineer' but I made some calls and I literally think he was the guy who worked the light switches.

Who knows, he might have made an excellent spaceman, but, as I say, it never got that far. They built a space shuttle suit of armor onto his body, 'as a test,' and then just before they lowered the helmet and brought out the roman candle, he lit up that nervous farewell cigarette.

A bespectacled doctor swam in the astronaut's vision. "It's not good. I'm looking at your chart here — *where's his chart?* Thank you nurse. Yeah, this looks terrible. I'm gonna level with you, tell it to you straight. *Damn, look at the size of that thing.* How have you been feelin' lately?"

The test pilot — you know what, as a mark of our narrative compassion we're just gonna award him the title of 'astronaut,' even if it *is* categorically inaccurate. As I was saying, the *astronaut* continued in a bleary voice. "I feel awful, Doc. Well — I can't feel a thing, really. My eyeballs hurt, and everything else feels like the skin on fried chicken."

The doctor nodded thoughtfully. "Oh yeah, the skin is the best part. All crispy. Nothing better."

"I think I feel blood — uh, blood pouring down everywhere."

"We've got you bandaged up pretty good, I'm sure it's nothing. You're on a lot of drugs. Everything we could find, really. *The works.* Your reaction time might be a little off, if you're even processing the words I'm saying at all."

The astronaut tried to sit up. "No, listen. This feels — different. Like I'm bleeding, *inside*. Like I'm just filling up."

"I wouldn't worry about it, son. Probably just the tumor. It's taking up most of your belly at this point. Like I told you, never seen one this big."

The astronaut's arms gave out, and he collapsed back onto the bed. "Oh god. Never? But it — I've been feeling fine. And isn't big good, anyway, like you can just cut it right out? A bigger target to hit?"

The doctor bit his lip with genuine academic curiosity. "You know, we tried that. While you were out. It's not a bad idea, you've got instinct. But uh — no, afraid not." He scoffed. "It fought back."

"But — you've got knives and scalpels, scissors! Get this thing out of me, Doc! Come on!"

The clipboard was shaking in the doctor's hand. "I think we're past that now. It looked pretty mean."

"Mean?"

"Yeah, it's developing quick. Getting hungry too. It'll eat the organs, but you've still got a couple hours. Lookin' at you, in profile, you look like you're expecting. Stretch marks up and down the torso, scarring — be grateful for the bandages. That thing is up to sixty-five pounds now!"

The astronaut opened and closed his mouth a few times.

"Doc?"

"What's up, son?"

"Where am I? What's going on here? Where are the other patients?"

The doctor put down the clipboard and started cleaning his glasses with his tie. "We've had to move you to a special unit. No tools in here either. It melted through the scalpel we used to open you up. Just broke it down and swallowed it up. Maybe don't move too quick, that blade might still be in there."

"You keep — you're talking crazy, Doc. Saying the wildest things I've ever heard like there's nothing wrong."

The doctor continued to grind away at his glasses, eager to avoid eye contact. "Well, I'm a professional. You deserve honesty and a cool head. And don't worry, we've — taken precautions."

"Precautions, that's good to hear! Do you take insurance?"

The doctor was scared to death. Petrified. Quaking in his rubber boots. They were in the basement of a hurriedly vacated military hospital, two days after the thermonuclear meltdown at the Apollo lab. The mid-interview test pilot had been declared dead at the scene, but when they tried to place his body on a stretcher, the metal support bars crackled with electricity and shocked the paramedics.

Another ambulance was called and a few more paramedics arrived with a few more stretchers. The siren blared to life when the stretchers were loaded in the back, but hey — weird stuff happens sometimes. And so what if the test pilot's body twitched or spasmed occasionally? Honestly, they just thought it was morning traffic the first few times it happened. But when they pried off the space shuttle walls and carved through the insulation, they saw a huge angry eyeball pressed against the man's seemingly lifeless body — blinking up at them and then squinting hatefully.

The body convulsed again, and this time they saw the electric shock blazing along his skin. The hospital was emptied out in record time, and as calls went out to the top two hundred *what-the-hell-is-this* doctors in the country, a crack squad of *real* scientists were brought in to insulate the premises. In an hour, the hospital had been fully encased in lead. In a day, the doctors had arrived and a good number of them had retired.

The astronaut closed his eyes hard. His brain sent out the signal for tears, but he started drooling instead. "Back there, in the lab, who else made it out?"

"You know, that's a really good question. We're gonna get someone on that. Good thinking, very considerate."

"Just me?"

The doctor put his glasses back on. They almost slid off again, he was sweating so much. "Well, you and uh — the tumor."

"What do we do about that, Doc? You said you were gonna tell it to me straight. When do you operate? Can we try radiation? Chemo?"

"I mean, we can grab a plastic fork and knife from the mess hall. Beyond that, it just eats anything metal. Or lights it up. Deep fried a few of my — predecessors, when they tried." He forced himself to meet the astronaut's eye, which had finally started to tear up. "You want the truth? We think it's alive, and it might have already shimmied up your spine and eaten your brain. You could be it and it could be you. Which means I'm talkin' to a tumor right now. Please don't kill me, I've been so nice."

The astronaut's mouth fell open, and it seemed like a voluntary gesture. "Well, I think it's definitely hit some nerve endings, because I accept the words that you just said." He raised a trembling finger. "But I do not accept your defeatism."

"Legally, you've already been dead for days. You died seven different times on the way here."

"One question for you, Doc."

The doctor shook his head. "No, we can't use porcelain knives. Already tried that. It eats *everything*. Unless I'm speaking to the tumor right now, in which case *you* eat everything. Which is impressive, actually. Unique. Really cool."

A moment of mutually baffled silence passed between them.

"Did I get the job?" The astronaut was almost smirking.

"I'm sorry, I don't know what you — "

"The test pilot technician role? It doesn't matter, I was in the suit and the accident happened in the workplace." He tried to sit up again. "My best buddy is a lawyer, I know how this works. Unless you want to spend the next couple years in court, you *have* to operate on me. I know my rights!"

He didn't, but as I say, the doctor was terrified. There were fifty assault rifles trained on the *one* door out of the impromptu operating room. If this thing got out, the whole world was gonna have a Problem on its hands.

And even still, as the doctor pulled a ballpoint pen out of his coat pocket to draft his letter of resignation, the tumor responded. Ballpoint pens, as you may know, have a little ball of metal lodged right there at the point. And metal, as you have just learned, is something of a *no-no* around the tumor, who interpreted this harmless, admittedly defeatist action as an act of war — the unsheathing of a blade. And so it reacted, violently.

"Hey — no, I'm your friend. Remember? *Lay back down!*"

The astronaut was drooling again. "I'm not doing anything. I think it's got my legs. Just put down the pen, maybe. I think it's — oh god, that wasn't me. Sorry."

The test pilot had not done it on purpose. Truthfully, he had not done it at all. The tumor had run the pilot's limp, floppy body over to the doctor, grabbed his pen, gouged out an eyeball, and then blasted a bolt of electricity directly into his brain — which then melted out of the recently vacated eyehole.

All of this happened so fast, and so *without* his involvement, that the pilot really only registered it as they started sprinting towards the heavily guarded exit door. He screamed bloody murder and fought for control of his limbs, but it was a losing battle. The tumor was pure survival instinct, an alchemical machine born out of the stew of flammable, explosive, toxic, and experimental doodads littered about the Apollo lab.

And the drugs weren't helping. It simply wasn't a fair fight. The pilot started to flatline, for the eighth time in two days, as they burst through the exit door and the soldiers opened fire. It was a tremendous blaze of muzzle flashes Tand polaroid shots of the pilot's twisted skeleton as the tumor mercilessly burned their way out of the hospital. They melted through the lead wall and crackled across the parking lot. The pilot was only dimly conscious of the hospital johnny flapping behind them as they sprinted and loped their way to freedom.

He put up a fight about a mile from the ocean. A chortling seagull stirred him to action, and in one brief flash of sanity, he saw the world-ending power of this creature that had taken root inside of him. And then the pilot did something brave. He sacrificed himself to save others, to take out the monstrous tumor and put an end to all of this before things really went sideways.

For just a minute, he managed to wrestle back control of his legs and steer them towards the sea. Consciousness and life were just starting to fade away into the corners of his embattled mind when he hit the ice cold water and dove. Their shared body sparked and fizzled against the tide, but despite his very best efforts, the test pilot could not drown. The tumor had clawed its way into every one of his major organs, and their final battleground was to be his lungs.

Their arms and legs shot straight out as another wave of lightning rattled across the pilot's bones. Every fish within a quarter mile was electrocuted and just slightly charred, but still tender enough to eat if you had a nice sauce and some light seasoning.

Somewhere in that murky abyss under the ocean, the tumor took control fully. They walked out of the ocean calmly and made for home, as the parasite put his hijacked mind to work coming up with an insidious new plan. And the pilot let him. *What else was he going to do?* He watched and listened, and bided his time until the tumor grew tired many hours later.

They settled into an armchair and had a nice big dinner, and then just as the tumor was falling asleep, purring against his heart, the pilot very gently directed the left arm to extend outwards for a much-needed stretch. But before it could retract and settle in for a long winter's nap, he fired off a simple command, and they jabbed a dirty fork deep into an outlet.

The whole neighborhood short-circuited. And then the tumor roared back to life and that *second* electrical firestorm knocked out most of the eastern seaboard. New wires were hung of course, and everyone got to go back to watching TV within just a few hours, but this unnatural disaster did catch the attention of the local police. From there, word spread to the military, who were very busy conducting an international manhunt for the escaped tumor monster.

It was all over very quickly after that, and one final precaution was taken. The test pilot and the tumor were locked in a little cage and fired out into the endless reaches of space. It was decided that if they were going to make a mess of things, then they could just as well make a mess *out there*, far, far away from impressionable voters.

This had to be done quietly, of course. No one could know that any of this had ever taken place. The Frankenstein birth, the imprisonment, the escape, the incompetence — the *optics* of this situation were terrible for everyone, especially that dearly departed doctor.

A two-tiered mission was hastily assembled. On the surface, this was to be just another launch, another valiant attempt at winning the space race. But strangely, they didn't even try to approach the moon. Mechanical failures suddenly and conveniently arose, and in the end, Apollo 11 was lucky to make it back in one piece.

But little did the enraptured public know, as their hearts soared with televised tales of heroism and adventure, that the *true objective* had been achieved quickly and silently out the back door — as a small, low-tech escape pod carrying the test pilot and the tumor was fired out of a large exhaust pipe. No one cared where they went, as long as it was away from Earth. Of course, there was very little insulation in the escape pod, and the journey through atmosphere is not a kind one.

The test pilot was almost jumbled to pieces by the extraordinary pressure and turbulence, and — well, just as they crossed out into open space his bowels gave way, and they were finally split in twain. The test pilot — very painfully but quite suddenly — pooped it out, and in the act of traveling at such supersonic speeds alongside blazing thrusters and the panting excesses of heat and unfiltered kinetic energy, the tumor was forever altered.

Meta-biological fissures were unbalanced and re-oxidized. Subatomic nucleotides evolved and de-phaser-fied. Put more simply, the malicious blob of bright orange goo heated up, burbled, and was remade at a cellular level. Put even more simply, it turned green.

Now, the official story is that none of this ever happened, that the Problem cannot be sourced back to Earth or the Apollo lab in any way. The officially sanctioned version of events tells us that the test pilot died in a freak accident during the waning days of the space race.

But, you know, who's to say? The official story also claims that we *eventually* landed on the moon, and that might actually be worse. All that trouble for some big dumb empty rock?

Let's hope there was more to it than that.

Chapter Three: <u>Moonshot</u>

What's the longest you've ever held your breath? Thirty seconds? For me, it's probably about a minute. Maybe ten, I wasn't counting. You drive by a skunk, you're standing at the urinal after some asparagus — it's a survival thing. You lock it down, for however long it takes to get to safety. But your focus is on the ungodly stench, not the passage of time. Unless, for example, there is no stench, and you're just choking to death, stranded in the unfeeling maw of open space.

Now, luckily, Captain Duncan Arugula was not quite that desperate — yet. He was still wearing his space suit, and of course, still vacuum-sealed inside the space oven that served as his impromptu escape pod from *The Clunker*. But he was still keenly aware, with every additional ragged breath, that things were not looking great.

Even worse, every time he tried to disassociate and tempt back whatever muse inspired his ingenious schemes, he would accidentally make eye contact with the Problem again. It was hard not to, his whole field of vision was just infinite cold nothing, the occasional blip of an exploding star, and one raging, gloopy green eyeball. It didn't have quite enough — *skin?* — left to blink, but the Problem was undoubtedly still alive. For one thing, it was still twitching, and that pupil was contracting ever tighter, narrowing to an impossibly small *dot* of the purest imaginable loathing.

This was becoming more than mere competition, some tired 'survival of the fittest' demonstration. The longer the staring contest went, the more *personal* this felt, for both of them. Much more of this and things would escalate into a full-blown rivalry.

A fuzzy, scratchy voice boomed through the space oven, bouncing off the walls and crackling through Duncan's skull. "Makin' one more pass. Once again, this is *The Apollo*. I'm seein' debris all over the damn place." The Captain didn't catch every word, there was too much distortion.

Some small, rational part of his brain observed that the voice sounded old and tired, and not at all amazed by the fate of *The Clunker*. "Looks like an engine explosion. No distress signals received so far. Any survivors out there, please radio in, local frequency. Final call. I'm circlin' one more time, then claimin' the scrap."

Now, it must be observed that Captain Arugula's flight suit was not outfitted with a radio, which was really too bad, given the circumstances. Fortunately for him, if not his eardrums, the complex metallic makeup of his floating tomb — the *top-of-the-line* space oven — was acting as something of a two-ton receiver, with the power cord becoming a cheeky, bootleg antenna.

Of course, this also meant that all those wiggly little sound waves really had nowhere to go once they made their way inside the oven. And so they bounced, reflected and refracted until they nearly deafened the poor Captain. And then he panicked, which sort of *compounded* the noise problem.

"Mayday! Mayday! Captain Arugula of *The Clunker* making contact. Code red! Help!"

As I say, he doesn't have a radio in the suit. *The Clunker* had one, but I'm not sure thermoblast annihilation is covered by the warranty. It appears the communication is, for now, one-way.

The disembodied voice continued in earnest, sounding suddenly and selfishly *chipper*. "Alright, that's my due diligence. Some of this looks valuable. Clearin' out the trash with some light artillery, then we get pickin'. Guns up!"

"*No, wait! I'm in here! I'm still here!*"

Time seemed to slow to a crawl. Duncan knew the guns were heating up. He knew the space oven wasn't bulletproof. And he knew, for real this time, that he was about to die. And so the Captain indulged himself, *one last time*. He had a lot of unresolved stress still rattling around inside him, and this latest apocalypse was simply too much.

"Is that all you see? *Scrap? Trash?*" His voice cracked, or maybe it was his brain? "This is my *home* you're turning your guns on! The only home I've ever known, the graveyard of all my friends — every single one of them! Clean sweep. But no, you have fun! Swiss cheese my entire life! Why not? Not much left now, is there? A couple bones, a wing, not even a coffin to put it in!"

He pounded the walls of the space oven with his fists, barely even feeling the pain. "And I'd *gladly* come out there and explain the whole situation in person, but there's a homicidal, flesh-ripping, sneezing, snarling, I-don't-know-what *parasite* keeping me trapped inside this kitchen appliance!"

In the heat of the moment, the Captain forgot himself, and swung open the oven door. "Come on, where is it? Let it rip, light me up — *show me what you got!*"

The Apollo still couldn't hear him, obviously, but that's not to say that this final flourish was not consequential. For one thing, the violent swing swung of the shiny metal oven door caught the stranger's eye. He squinted through a wasteland of scorched metal — *there he was* — an apoplectic space captain emerging from some sort of tiny square escape pod. Or was it a washing machine? Very industrious of him, in any case.

But that wasn't all. While Captain Arugula was catching his breath, the oven door lazily swung back around. And through the glass, he saw *The Apollo's* 'light artillery' roaring to life. It hit him too late, a quiet realization that scared him even more than the machine guns or the cannons.

But before Duncan could well and truly panic, the voice over the radio made contact again. *"What the hell you doin' out there? I radio'd, I waited, I've been runnin' laps over here tryin' to save your life! Wait* — hold on now."* The Apollo* came to a sudden stop.

"Your radio ain't workin', that right?"

Captain Arugula nodded.

"Well then, we're gonna do this real simple. One question. Answer right, welcome aboard. Answer wrong?" He let the moment linger, and his voice was *different* the next time he spoke. More relaxed. More dangerous. "You see, I'm a man on a mission. And there ain't enough time left for loose ends."

"Understood, Captain. Loud and clear." Duncan's voice was muffled through the glass of the space over door, but then again — *who knows, maybe the stranger was a lip reader?* Just to cover all his bases, Captain Arugula also gave a quick thumbs up and saluted.

But *The Apollo* was all business, slow and clear, impossible to misunderstand or misinterpret. "Have you encountered the creature?"

Something coiled tight inside Duncan's stomach as he shook his head and tried to look confused. "No, no I don't think so! Just engine failure. Bad luck!"

"That's a relief. Good to hear. Gimme a second, I'll swing around, come get you. Last thing, just gotta say it so it's out there. If you're lyin' to me, I'll find out and I'll throw you into the furnace that powers the ship. Liars ain't worth a damn, and fuel ain't cheap."

Captain Arugula watched *The Apollo* deftly maneuver through the minefield of his own destroyed ship with a toxic blend of jealousy and dread. Wherever that accursed eyeball had escaped to, it might well return, and he would need help killing it when it did. He tried to think positively — maybe it really was dead, flung lightyears out into open space when he'd thrown open the oven door — but then another member of his crew floated by. He couldn't tell who it was without the skin, but they looked *familiar enough.*

The disembodied Captain of *The Apollo* jolted him back to reality. "Bad news, I'm afraid. Engineerin' problem, from all this garbage floating around. Visitor's entrance is jammed. Took a beatin' in the blast!"

Captain Arugula tried once more to think positively, but the closest he could get was a *brief* mental breakdown. He bent his elbow and wrist as hard as they could go and pointed his hand towards his face. His fingers bunched up, and he heard his own haughty voice as though from a great distance.

"Mister Swan, I have simply had enough of all this. Today has gone on long enough, and I'm taking action! A few options: one, I unlatch my helmet and rejoin my crew. Two, nap time. Maybe things will be different after a good rest. Three, you grow some wings and fly us to safety. *Your call!"*

His hand didn't move. Captain Arugula waited, staring darkly at his trembling featherless hand, reaching deep within himself to find the patience. The resolve. The inner peace. But *still,* the swan said nothing.

The voice over the radio cut in uncertainly. "Hey, uh — stranger? You doin' alright?"

Duncan ignored the spaceship that kept referring to his life's work with the language of the landfill, and raised his eyebrows at Mister Swan. "It is an honor, to be entrusted with the Captain's confidence. To be asked for input, it's unheard of for such a new recruit! But please don't do me the indignity of wasting my time. The helmet, the power nap, or the wings?"

Something strange happened then. It might have been a trick of the light, as *The Apollo* turned on the high beams to get his attention, or it might have been real. The swan turned its head to gaze back at the space oven, and deep inside his mind, it answered Duncan's question. The idea fell out of nowhere and clicked neatly into place. It was a brilliant, ingenious plan. The Captain saluted once more, and the swan departed.

The Apollo, of course, was still there, watching the whole time. "The *hell* you doin' down there?"

Captain Duncan Arugula had not been spoken to this way in quite some time, but he found it oddly refreshing. They weren't competitors ruffling their feathers, they were equals — *they were pirate brethren.* Scurvy dogs working together to battle the high seas.

He flapped his arms up and down like he was landing a plane, and then pointed dramatically at the moon. The Captain of *The Apollo* may have responded, but if he did, Duncan never heard it. This was going to be a difficult flight, he needed to concentrate. Before he climbed back into the space oven, Duncan ripped the lifeless power cord out of the back of the equally lifeless appliance — and for some complicated scientific reason that we simply don't have time to explain, that worked. The string was cut, and the tin cans returned to their respective corners.

A moment of silence and preparation, a thorough systems check, and then both Captains set sail.

"Alright, easy does it. Gonna curl up in here, just for a second, get some momentum going. *Bit of a squeeze,* that's okay." Duncan resented the sudden strain as his voice shifted to a higher pitch. "Just have to pretzel up a little, make things more aerodynamic. And here we go!"

He started flapping the space oven door open and closed with increasing vigor. With his other hand, he held onto a large piece of the hull that had bumped into them during the 'Mister Swan' interlude. The oven began to rotate slowly, and then faster as he continued to build kinetic energy. If you've ever seen one of those accordion blowy things they use to get fireplaces all worked up — well, it's nothing like that.

When the oven was well and truly worked up into a spin cycle, Captain Arugula pushed off as hard as he could from the hull, and threw the door all the way open. He shot away from the wreckage, trailing magnificently behind *The Apollo*, which — you know — had engines.

"There we go, like a champagne cork into the moonlight. And now we stabilize, pop my head out to chart a course — old school navigation, *analogue* — and make a few adjustments." He squinted into eternity with a weathered eye. "A door is whatever you want it to be. A mudflap, a top sail, and in a pinch, a pretty good pair of *wings*. Much obliged to my first mate for that one. He's making a wonderful first impression."

The Apollo landed gracefully on the surface of the stupid ass moon. Thick streams of exhaust shot out the sides. Spindly landing gear emerged from chic little panels. A staircase even unfolded from the cockpit. Genuine computing equipment conducted initial scans of the surface and started to look for signs of life. It was all very impressive.

Captain Arugula, meanwhile, came sailing in on a hollowed out convection oven. He didn't have any brakes, of course, but that's okay.

The surface of the moon is already a mess, no one's gonna notice a few extra divots.

"Hey, kid, that was some damn good flyin' you did back there! Glad you made it out."

But Duncan wasn't ready for pleasantries just yet. "*Just give me a second, please.*" He locked his heels and placed his hand on his heart. "Dearly beloved, we are gathered here today because — everybody died." He looked out at the stars, but they didn't give him any of the usual comfort. "Everybody except me. My ship is gone now too, officially, with the loss of this fine piece of machinery."

"If I may — what was her name?"

Duncan took a knee, looking past the wreckage of the space oven. "Of course, fellow pirate. She was called *The Clunker*, and I was her proud Captain for more than fifteen years. She was my home."

"A good long run, over too soon. My condolences."

As one, and unbidden, they saluted. The knob that had once controlled the 'broil' setting on the space oven popped off and floated away, setting off on a ten-thousand-year-long journey that would end in the fiery vortex of an exploding star.

Duncan stood, collecting himself. "Thank you for that."

"My pleasure, I've been there. Hard, losin' everyone."

Captain Arugula turned around to face the stranger. He was old, possibly very old, but cavalier. You could tell that he'd been on his own for a long time. Makeshift bandana on his head, the kind of smirk that takes years to form — and never quite goes away. He was a Captain's Captain, and when you added in his *clear* seniority, a chain of command began to emerge.

"Nice to meet you. I am Duncan Arugula, the — *former* Captain of *The Clunker*."

The stranger extended a hand. "As I say, a pleasure. You can call me Frank. *The Apollo*'s my ship, even if it ain't much of one. Built it myself, out of whatever I could find. Wrecks, leftovers, scrap, spare parts. Took a long time, but it flies."

Never in his entire life had Duncan Arugula been so impressed. He allowed himself a single glance to survey the ship, eyebrows carefully furrowed the whole time. It was a marvel, a revelation, every inch a towering monument to sheer force of will and mechanical inspiration.

"Nice ship."

His mind had gone completely blank, awash in self-loathing and admiration. He panicked and changed the subject.

"You know, I've never been to the moon this time of year. Looks nice." Is that all he could say? *Nice?* Nice ship, nice moon, no wonder he was gonna end up being this guy's latrine cadet.

Frank shrugged. "Never had the pleasure, myself. Ain't been anyone here in a long time."

"I'm sorry to make you go out of your way. I'm happy to work off the debt, uh — the price of the fuel."

Frank waved him away. "Nonsense. Might be something worthwhile on this godforsaken rock after all. We're here now, it's worth a look. Personally I'm excited to what all the fuss was about."

Duncan sighed, quietly relieved. He would've offered to just pay the guy, but he was pretty sure he'd left his wallet where he always left it — on *The Clunker*. "Nice plan. Very nice. Uh — I mean, what is it we're looking for?"

"Munitions, primarily. And I don't mean bullets." Frank's eyes narrowed with excitement. "Heat rays, solar cells, vaporizers, anythin' you can use to barbecue a beast."

"Oh wow, that's funny, I'm sort of a foodie too. More of a baker, I guess, but still!"

Frank glanced back at Duncan with a confused grimace. "I was speakin' metaphorical, actually. But that's nice to know. I can't cook for shit. I eat it whole, whatever it is."

"Huh! *How efficient!* That would save some time, I imagine." Duncan could feel himself panicking, but he couldn't seem to stop the words coming out of his mouth. "No spices, no simmering, no finicky family recipes. Awash in aromatic memories, absently stirring the nostalgia — oh God, they're all gone."

In a flash, the elder Captain threw him up against the side of *The Apollo*. "We're gettin' along real nice so far, but I gotta make sure your head's on straight. We could be walkin' into a trap here, a *slaughter!* You best get your mind outta the pantry and focus on the objective, soldier. Munitions. Survival. Intelligence."

The sudden impact brought Duncan back to himself. "Unhand me, grandpa, and do not mistake my misty-eyed melancholy for weakness. I harbor a blood feud with this — *place?*" He caught himself, just barely. Lucky for him, Frank mistook Duncan's emotional baggage for his own, and released him.

"I hear you. Apologies. I've got history with 'this place' too. Swore I'd never come here, *never*, after what they did to me." He backed up, and fixed his rumpled spacesuit.

"But here I am, a bonafide astronaut, walkin' on the moon."

"What do *you* have against — the moon?"

Something beeped inside the ship and Frank straightened up. "We're not safe here. Let's go, talk on the way." He hesitated. "You got a gun?"

"Not anymore, no."

"Just as well. Hold on a sec."

Frank dashed back inside *The Apollo* and emerged again not ten seconds later. Duncan was stunned by the older man's agility, and even more surprised when he handed him — "A heat ray. In case we encounter the creature."

Duncan tried to keep his voice level. "This is a hair dryer."

"Ha! It *was* a hair dryer. Amazing what happens when you put the batteries in backwards." Frank scoffed at his own brilliance. "Cross a few wires, couple modifications, that thing'll burn you alive from the inside out. Liquify your eyeballs, tenderize your organs, thin your blood. Hell, you get a get a good bead on 'im, maybe he'll even change color again. Who knows what comes after green?"

With a nod of thanks, Duncan gingerly took possession of the hair dryer. That was confirmation. The creature *was* the Problem, and now he had officially lied to this nimble, well-armed old man, who had not just threatened but *promised* to kill him if he ever found out. He heard the plastic handle of the hair dryer creak and tried to relax his grip.

Frank didn't seem to notice. "Come on now." Without looking back, he pressed a button on his keys and locked *The Apollo*. "Earlier, you asked about the moon. How much do you know?" He darted forward across the rubble, leading them deftly through an asteroid shower of twisted *Clunker* parts.

"Uh, about the moon? Just the broad strokes. Grey. Patchy. No atmosphere, not much gravity. No water. No life." Duncan shrugged, wondering if this was some sort of test. "It's just a boulder with a flag stuck in it."

Frank nodded thoughtfully. "So your blood feud, it's with the moon or the flag? I can't tell from the debris — or your suit — was *The Clunker* a military ship?"

Duncan stood up a little straighter. "No sir, not officially, but we ran some jobs for them over the years."

"A man of intrigue. I'll bite. *Watch it, engine coming in on your starboard flank.*" Frank grabbed for Duncan's arm just as the Clunker's jagged, broken windshield cratered into the ground between them. He didn't lose the arm, but a few layers of flesh were shaved off like deli-fresh roast beef.

"Frank! *Ah!* Are you alright?"

Frank grumbled through clenched teeth. It looked bad.

"This is ridiculous. I'm bringing you back to the ship, right now. You can scavenge the moon some other time. It's too dangerous out here!"

Duncan could tell that Frank was muzzling himself, trying to ignore the pain, but the amount of profanity in his grumblings was steadily increasing.

"You're in shock, don't talk. Give me your other arm, there you go. Just lean on me, you're gonna be fine."

Frank wrenched his jaw open. "*No, wait — look!*"

Duncan kept his focus. "I know. It's my ship, trust me, I know all of it. Every rusted screw. Please, focus on walking — and put some pressure on that wound."

"Shut up, Dunko!" Frank made a woozy noise that reminded Duncan of a water buffalo he'd seen at the zoo during his youth. "Look at this!"

Duncan ducked underneath a fragment of fuselage and turned back to look. Frank was pointing a shaking finger at what looked like some sort of ruined golf cart. "It's true, they made it! But when? How? I would have picked them up on the — " He shut his eyes against a fresh wave of nerve pain. "Are you seein' this too?"

"Yeah, I think so. It's all busted up, but those antennas — that's a 'lunar lander'." Duncan's eyebrows shot up. "You think it still runs?"

Frank fell to his knees and crawled over to the vehicle. "Might be, if I just — damnit! It's shot to hell. Tires are blown, axle's all bent up." With his good arm, Frank wiped away some dust and grime. "Blaster holes. Duncan, run! Take my keys, get back to *The Apollo!*"

"What? No!" Duncan spun around, looking for threats.

"That's an order! Leave me, I'll be fine! The creature could still be here!"

Duncan threw his hands into the air, cursing this *endless* day. "I'm not leaving you! Come on, get up! Give me your arm."

Frank grabbed Duncan's face. His bottom lip was quivering, but his eyes blazed with clarity and confidence. "One of us has to make it!" He was steeling himself against the pain, but his hands were shaking with fear. "You listen to me, soldier. Guns up. Hostiles inbound. Position compromised. Regroup at *The Apollo.*"

He winced, reaching into his bloodstained spacesuit. "Take this, and leave me the heat ray."

Duncan reached down and took the weapon. It looked like a sawed-off shotgun. From everything he'd learned about this strange, rogue Captain, he'd probably sawed it off himself. And who knows what he'd done to the bullets!

Both of their heads popped up as a distant, excited, *telltale* gurgle reached them. Duncan grabbed Frank's shoulder and stared into his eyes, suddenly fierce and focused.

"I'm coming back for you."

"Damn straight — now run!"

Chapter Four: <u>Arms Race</u>

Trench warfare just *sounds* unpleasant, doesn't it? *Trench*, now there's an ugly word. You've got that arachnid undertone, the grumble in the middle, it's unwieldy on the tongue. What is a trench anyway? A half-ass tunnel? Some sort of slide? Am I playin' army man here or doin' the *luge?*

And then there's the prospect of getting stuck with a bayonet. No thank you. But what's the alternative? Tens of thousands of cold, hungry soldiers slamming into each other and ruining a perfectly nice meadow. It only gets worse from there. Submarines that look like zebras. Suits of armor. Drummers, presumably in charge of morale? Horses wearing big x-ray bibs. I'm sure they're doing stuff with robots now too. *The armies, not the horses.*

And then there's whatever the hell the Redcoats were up to! Doin' a dose-doe in little cliques. That's it boys, a few more *sashes* should win the war. But underneath it all, literally, is the real nightmare. These fields, *trenches,* castle courtyards and town squares — they're all absolute *hotbeds* of mud.

Unspeakably dirty conditions. The crust, the filth, the bugs. *The mud.*

None of this occurred to Frank, as he hobbled and dodged his way through the maelstrom. Too busy fighting for his life, I guess, he didn't stop for a single moment to appreciate that the moon — for all its faults — was entirely mud-free.

"Son of a bitch that hurts!" Frank gritted his teeth and pushed forward, listening hard for signs of the creature. "Just like last time, eh? Better out than in!"

He withdrew *another* sawed-off shotgun from within his salvaged spacesuit. Impressive storage capacity on that thing. It looked like — well, like a secondhand bomber jacket he peeled off a corpse — but maybe that was the point. He'd been waiting for this rematch for years. Who knows how many strategic little pockets and secrets he sewed into the lining?

"I wonder — do you still glow in the dark? *I do.*" He squinted against an explosion of glass as more *Clunker* parts crashed down around him. The creature was here, he knew it. *He could feel it.* Their hunting patterns were remarkably similar. And how could it resist the allure, the intoxicating aroma of his —

"Blood. If he wasn't on to me before, he sure as shit is now. Not a bad way to draw him out, actually. Unless I bleed to death first."

Frank stumbled to one side as an engine block blew a crater into the useless patch of moon *previously known* as the 'Sea of Tranquility.'

His head was spinning. The moon was spinning. Frank groaned and tried to catch himself, but he fell to his knees — and it all started to fade away. "No, damn you. Not yet!"

Inspiration struck him like a chef with an empty fridge. The cupboards were bare, but he had to eat *something,* so his perspective shifted. Everything became an ingredient, or in this case, a tool. Hunger sharpened his mind. Desperation honed his senses.

"Smells like bacon." Frank looked around curiously. His stomach was growling like a caged animal. Why would there be fresh bacon on the moon? He *was* hungry. No, he was bleeding, and he'd blacked out. Frank's stomach did a backflip as he looked down, and understanding broke through the fog of metaphor.

He switched off the heat ray and returned it to his belt, and then he touched his arm *very gingerly.* "Smart thinkin', Cap, but it stinks like hell."

He grimaced. When talking to oneself, was one supposed to play both sides of the conversation, or was it more of a continuous monologue? As he stalled out on this question, and wondered if he was broiling any other parts of his body right now, Frank's eyes came back into focus.

He'd thought it was just a dent, a divot, another pockmark scarring up this hopeless rock. But no — this was something else entirely. He crawled over and lifted it up, and only then did he believe it. "A manhole cover, marked with Russian characters. Hmm."

Frank could not read Russian.

"At times like these, wish I could read Russian."

As I say, he was not fluent in the language.

"Never really considered it before. Didn't seem like I was missin' out on much, to be frank."

He slapped his own knee, in English.

"Buncha miserable books, thick as a brick. Nah, I'm good. And the vodka, the paintings — presumably more sad shit — they're sorta pre-translated. Universal-like. But right now — "

He trailed off, lost in the great mystery of things. It wasn't that complicated, really, he had gone for that test pilot interview during the Cold War. It was around then, anyway. Back then, they were pulling the red out of the crayon box. Of course he didn't know Russian.

"Good on 'em, I suppose, makin' it here in the end. The bastards." He cocked his head to one side. "Still, it's an unusual thing to pack. What were the odds this place was gonna have sewers?" He looked around, struck by a sudden hunch.

"You know, now that I think of it — I see a flagpole. Old Glory, all tattered up. Might borrow that for *The Apollo*." He leaned back, reclining in zero gravity. "Besides that though, ain't jack shit anywhere. Nothin' and no one."

A far off, famished growl broke the silence. Frank cocked the shotgun and smiled. "All in good time." And with a smirk, he popped open the manhole cover.

On the other side of the wreckage — the business end — *former* Captain Duncan Arugula was having a hell of a time trying to board *The Apollo*. He could feel the momentum of the moment slipping away. It's difficult to make a clean getaway without a getaway *car* — at the very least, it makes things more difficult for the driver.

"Take the keys, take this — I don't know, is this some kind of *trench* gun? He's old as dirt, who knows which war he served in!" Duncan was muttering and spluttering, getting himself all worked up. "Asking me about *The Clunker* like that, he was sneering, that's what he was doing. Sneering. Knows damn well it wasn't a military ship. He knows I didn't build it myself from mothballs and battery acid like he did. Oh but let's all look at *The Apollo!*"

He swung his arms around a little bit, fully shadowboxing now. "A bit *ostentatious* for the name of a ramshackle old — yeah, exactly! A — ramshackle. *The Ramshackle*, there's a spaceship name for ya! And where is he, Captain Dinosaur — oh right, he's very busy prowling around the moon looking for more hair dryers. And then there's me — "

He tore the Captain's pin off his chest — one of those little plastic paint swatches they spackle all over uniforms — and threw it into the void. Of course, in the serenity of zero gravity, it just kind of floated next to him for a while, and then started meekly bumping into things.

"Me — the aspiring latrine cadet who's spent the last ten minutes of my evaporating life looking for where I'm supposed to stick these keys. In the door? You'd think so, wouldn't you? But I guess that was just too cliche for the genius designer. Maybe in the exhaust pipe, or — or — *I don't know!*"

He kicked the ship. It was an ungracious gesture, made even more so by the shameful molasses of the moon's pathetic atmosphere.

Fortunately for Duncan, it worked, and the visitor's entrance door sprang open.

He couldn't believe it, but the thrill of something going *right* buoyed his mood, and helped him process the unique agony of boarding a ship for the first time since losing *The Clunker*.

"It really is a nice ship. Cozy, but not lazy. Visually interesting without being too busy. Modern, but not futuristic. Industrial, never utilitarian. No pastiche. This is an old sports car. A restoration job." He shook his head and smiled. "A classic. Exactly what you need and nothing more. Small flight deck, a few bunks, couple closets, oh and would you look at this?"

He drifted over to a brushed metal doorway that opened into a cramped, hastily upholstered gunner seat. Glass panels notched together overhead, reflecting the glowing green readout of a vintage targeting system. There were knobs everywhere, dimly flashing lights and worn-down buttons that called to him like buck-naked Greek sirens. It was the most beautiful thing Duncan Arugula had ever seen.

"The concrete practicality of iron sights, the classic cool of a punch throttle, the subtle patina on the leather armrests, the — god above, are those Triple Watt 95 recommissioned light force laser cannons?"

They were, if he says they were. Seems like he knows what he's talking about, we'll just go with it. Duncan continued jealously snooping through the ship, somewhat forgetting the urgency of this *rescue mission*. After his second pass through the bunks, some small part of him realized that he was avoiding the flight deck. It was still too much.

"I wonder what's in these closets! Could be essential."

With much gusto, he threw open the first closet door, which turned out not to be a closet at all. It was a small room, arguably something closer to a nest or a lair. Let's just say that it was the kind of door that you definitely put a lock on.

"Oh no." Duncan took half a step back. The room was a study. Or perhaps it was more of an *obsession*. A shrine of sorts, to the perilous, gelatinous 'creature' that was ruining both of their lives. One entire wall was dominated by a map of the solar system. It was a frantic crisscross of red yarn and push pins, a bowl of spaghetti thrown at the wall — a portrait of paranoia.

"Where did he find red yarn out here? And so much of it too. Ah!" He lashed out with a weird little flailing punch. Pure instinct. But this Problem wasn't a threat, not anymore. Duncan had seen something move out of the corner of his eye — a gloopy, gloppy shuffle into frame. He lowered his fists and cocked his head to one side.

"Oh, Frank. What have you been up to?" There were half a dozen of 'em, lined up on the shelf. Problems, suspended in some horrible goo and locked up in jars, all glooping and glopping and glowering down at him.

"Are they — "

He trailed off, and leveled the shotgun at the nearest jar.

"Were they ever really alive? *Parasites,* that's all they are. *How do you kill a parasite?*" He tried to meet the monster's gaze. "Well, they've got nothing to eat in there, no prey, no host — "

He cocked the shotgun.

"And yet, there they are."

If looks could kill, Duncan Arugula would first be ground down to a powder-fine subatomic schmutz, and then burned up with a fine baker's blowtorch, inhaled through spiteful nostrils, and finally, loogie'd into the bowels of an active nuclear reactor.

"Yeah, your brother felt the same way. Last time I saw him — he wasn't lookin' so good. Just an eyeball stuck on the side of my space oven. Who knows where he floated off to? With any luck, he was sucked into an engine. Burned up in some second rate atmosphere. Or

maybe he's just floating away, *hopeless.*
Helpless. Moseying into eternity without
eyelids to blink. Without a moment's
distraction or rest. Watching everything just
— "

He let the muzzle tap against the jar.
"Slip away."

His eyes swept over the rest of Frank's
trophy room. There were piles of printouts and
data readings, hand-written notes and
historical documents — frayed at the edges
where they'd been torn out of books. Other
walls were marked up with plans and strategies.
Most everything was crossed out, sometimes
quite violently. A lot of ink had been bled
across this room.

He could feel the rhythmic jostle of
Frank pacing back and forth, hear him muttering
to himself, feel the constant glances over at
the jars.

"It would almost be worth it."

He lowered the shotgun, and Duncan began
to pace, walking the very path where Frank had
wiled away so many years. The jars, the map,
the plans. They swirled around him, faster and
faster, until his mind caught on three little
words. He stopped dead and turned back to read
them again.

At the bottom of a long, winding list of
creative, crossed-out kills, was an idea that

Frank seemed to have settled on. It was circled, ground into the wall a hundred times over. Duncan gasped, and then the thing with the hair dryers kind of started to made sense.

"Burn 'em out."

It wasn't the first time that these grim words had been uttered on the moon. Decades earlier, as the space race was winding down, fears of nuclear annihilation were winding up. This was many years after that unfortunate incident with the test pilot and the tumor, let's call it *late* Cold War era. Not my area of expertise, if we're being honest. Hair metal, Reagan, sure — but beyond that, it's just static. The Bay of Pigs, when was that? And how did they even get involved? Livestock rarely take a side in geopolitics. Was this a group of particular bloodthirsty pigs — *baying* for blood — or were they occupying some contested body of water? As I say, this is somewhat outside my wheelhouse, tucked away in a dusty little shed of forbidden pig knowledge. I confess that I don't even know if they were American or Russian pigs.

Anyway, it was launch day for the final Apollo mission — no, wait. We can puzzle this out, *easily*. The classic American breakfast, *bacon* and eggs. Classic Russian breakfast — they're a husky people. You've got vodka, obviously, and tea rooms, but they must eat too. Huge land mass, lots of snow. Possible ice fishing. Do cows and chickens like the cold? I doubt it.

At the very least, they'd migrate somewhere warmer for the winter. That means no chickens year-round. No chickens means no eggs. But pigs are more *resilient* animals, less fussy than chickens. There must be a few sturdy Russian pigs — but again, not enough for a regular supply of bacon. Maybe oatmeal then? Water, oats, an old wooden bowl. Good Soviet slop, easy and consistent. Oats don't have summer homes. Alright then, maybe some ice fish for dinner? And potatoes will grow anywhere.

Yeah, that settles it. The pigs were American, and I can't think of any notable 'bays' anywhere — never mind the fact that your average hog definitely doesn't have access to swimming lessons — I'm gonna say this was about foreign policy. The baying of pigs, could have been a land grab, an invasion, gentrifying some industrial farming operation —

Point is, the eighties. The Apollo program launches its final mission. It's a back-up plan, a hush hush hail Mary. Apollo 38. You've probably never heard of it, and that was part of the plan. No press coverage, and the launch was officially branded a 'test' — which it was, sort of. If the Russians won the Cold War, or if anyone knocked over that first domino and blew up the planet, we'd need somewhere to go.

The moon was the obvious choice, because fuel was expensive and most of the program's budget had been used up by the first thirty-seven Apollo iterations. A couple dozen brave and brilliant Americans were strapped into the best rocket they could find and fired off to start a colony. When they landed — the Apollo team had gotten *substantially* better at that part over time — they started to unpack, and set up camp.

This is when things began to take a turn. There was *some* food in the rocket's pantry, a few pounds of dirt and a packet of seeds, but most of the cargo hold was filled up with rather *ambitious* building materials. Lots of iron gates and girders, piles of old doorknobs and porthole windows — but no nails. Not a single stick of glue or caulk or that fancy mashed potato mush they use on bricks.

The astronauts embraced the challenge and set about building what ended up looking like a bunch of camping tents. More than a few of these 'tents' collapsed during the first night. A few of the survivors marched off into the unknown looking for natural resources, some sort of ingenious moon adhesive — but they never came back. Everyone else fought over the remaining dirt — the seeds were long gone — and then, at long last, someone had to poop.

With a renewed sense of purpose, the astronauts gathered to dig tunnels for plumbing and irrigation. The cause became more and more *urgent* as the astronauts' stomachs started to break down the dirt, and soon enough they'd broken through the moon's outer crust.

And that was when things *really* started to take a turn, because those astronauts that had wandered off looking for moon glue had not just disappeared — they had been eaten. Picked clean, down to the marrow and eyelashes.

At that time, there were more than a few Problems roaming our measly corner of the galaxy, and the great majority of them had taken up residence on the same measly grey moon. It was thought to be abandoned, *open for business*, and so it was until the Apollo 38 astronauts started eating dirt.

Problems, as our aggrieved Captains have learned, tend to burrow and fester when they're ignored, or allowed to live. They pulse and spark and gurgle and swell up to become unmitigated disasters.

And the nest of Problems that were coiled up at the center of the moon were some of the most potent I have ever seen. The most acidic, wretched electric green mass, all throbbing and gnashing together — the heat built up so much that some of them started to turn orange again, and regrow human limbs. Fragments of Frank sprang up and rotted away, piling up under the outer crust. None of them got to a real *larval* stage, but wouldn't that have been fun?

You know what wasn't fun? The geyser of carnage incited by the faint scratching of a few constipated astronaut shovels. The Problems erupted through the death highways that the Apollo 38 crew had just built for them and boy did they *get to work*. Tore right though the space suits, ripped apart every last camping tent, and even took a few disrespectful victory laps. They didn't need to eat the doorknobs, that was excessive.

A few telltale helmets floated back to Earth, but unfortunately, they burned up in the atmosphere before they could crash down to the surface. No, I'm afraid that the tragic omens flowed in the other direction. As the final astronaut bled out, and admired the unexpected view of his own ribcage, the ship's radio squawked to life.

"HOUSTON TO APOLLO 38. COME IN APOLLO 38. CONFIRM CONTACT. CODE RED. CODE RED. I REPEAT — OH GOD, WHAT IF THEY'RE UP THERE TOO? APOLLO 38, CONFIRM CONTACT. WE'VE BEEN ATTACKED, THE WHOLE PLANET IS — *RADIO IN THE SECOND YOU GET THIS*. WE'RE DOING EVERYTHING WE CAN DOWN HERE. READY THE COLONY, PRIORITY NUMBER ONE. YOU'RE

ABOUT TO BE SLAMMED WITH ARRIVALS. EVAC ORDERS, GLOBAL. I REPEAT, READY THE COLONY. WE ARE ON OUR WAY. EVERYTHING WITH WINGS IS HEADED IN YOUR DIRECTION. MY FLIGHT IS IN AN HOUR, THIS IS A KITCHEN SINK JOB, WE ARE ALL GOING. STAY SAFE UP THERE, AND HEY, SAVE ME A COT? *DAMNIT, NO!* BAR THE DOOR! SHOOT IT, I DON'T KNOW!"

The signal collapsed in a rush of static. The Problems tucked in for some leftovers. And the last astronaut's brain finally realized that he was dead. The Cold War ended in the icy nothing of outer space, as the Americans' last best hush hush hail Mary plan fell to pieces — pieces that the Problems would comfortably consider *bite-sized*.

It was a day of vicious feasting across the surface of Earth and its pathetic moon too, and when the Problems were nice and bloated, they rolled and drooled their way back to bed.

In the case of the moon, this means that they retreated through the irrigation tunnels into their nest and settled in for a good long nap — undisturbed by anyone or anything for several blissful decades, until a certain grizzled Captain went snooping around looking for heat rays and hair dryers.

Chapter Five: <u>Tunnel Vision</u>

Frank was well and truly lost. He would never admit this, certainly not to young Duncan, but about three turns back — or maybe it was four — his mental map had started to fold in on itself, twisting and inverting until he walked headlong into a tunnel wall. He searched for it again in a desperate haze, flipping through useless happy memories and old Apollo designs.

Halfway through his childhood, Frank spotted something, and dove at it. A sudden cacophony cluttered his mind, a frantic and terrified sound.

Ribbit!

He slapped a few controls on his suit and a floodlight filled the tunnel. There was nothing there, nothing beyond dull grey rock and hack marks from ancient, unseen shovels.

"Aw hell! Where'd the sunuvabitch run off to? Can't see for shit down here, naturally. Gonna die in an extraterrestrial goddamn parking garage."

His eyes burned in the sudden light. "And then that two-bit nothin' is gonna take *The Apollo.*" His lips curled into a snarl. "Can't have that. Knew there was somethin' off with him. *I'm coming back for you.* Sure you are, kid. Sure you are."

Frank rallied and shut his eyes. That map was in here somewhere, skulking behind some family chili recipe or —

RIBBIT!

There it was, in the farthest corner of his mind, cowering in the basket of his very first bicycle. Frank reached out to grab it, and the map hopped into his outstretched hand with a grumbling blurp.

Ribbit! Ribbet, ribbet.

In the snowglobing of his confused brain, the tunnel map had been folded up into a slightly frayed and nervous origami frog. Frank didn't know quite what to do in this situation, but instinct told him to comfort the frog — and so he did.

Rrrribbit. Trrrry not to die down herrrre!

The frog unfolded in his hand, revealing a complex lattice of tunnels that, when viewed topographically, looked like an intricately cross-hatched drawing of a frowny face.

"Looks like my fuckin' biopsy results. Thanks, Brain Frog."

He was more right than he could possibly know, but we'll get to that soon enough. Frank's moment of melancholy was interrupted by a horrible grumbling noise that he almost convinced himself was coming from his own stomach. He cleared his throat to cover the sound and squinted harder at the map.

One of the eyes was larger than the other. More spidery tangles and offshoots. He ran a finger across the map, connecting more and more tunnel exits back to that swollen left eye. Somewhere in his mind, the frog purred again. It was a dreadfully throaty noise, texture like an asphalt runway. Frank's eyes rattled in their sockets.

"Now we're gettin' somewhere."

He took a moment to study the map, and then folded it back up into a frog and nudged it encouragingly. "Go on now. Be free. Roam. And if you see any bugs or anythin' — eat up. Make sure you get 'em all."

A shudder of self-awareness jolted through Frank. He wasn't just talking to himself anymore, this was something else entirely. As his late mother would say, *some real cuckoo shit.* Frank broke into a jog, literally attempting to run from these thoughts. He took corner after corner, climbed and slid, and tried to prepare himself for whatever fresh horror he would find in the left eyeball of the moon.

"Sweet jumpin' sarsaparilla — what now?"

Out of the distant shadow had extended a hand. It seemed to beckon him forward, and then wave, and stop dead — all in quick succession.

"What's that? You friend or foe?"

He quietly reached for the shotgun in his suit as the hand started to walk away, bobbing back into the lunar abyss. With a sigh, Frank followed it. "Dammit, here we go — guns up!"

And he buried both barrels into the sleepy green Problem that was crawling along the ceiling. The limp, vestigial arm flew off its body and clattered to the ground. It had the very same telltale birthmark on the elbow that Frank's did. He saw it immediately and started digging for more shells.

When the buckshot made contact, the Problem had split into a dozen little Problems. They were rolling like marbles, tumbling away to safety. He saw flashes of broken teeth and wild eyes, and then he remembered — and switched pockets. There was a special ammo pouch around here somewhere that he'd been just *waitin'* to try out.

"Runnin' away now? That's a new one!" He laughed cruelly, and it was those mocking guffaws that really made a mess of things. They ricocheted after the shotgun blasts, and caught up by the time the sound waves reached the nest. Together, the violent amplitudes of

Frank's arrival were just enough to wake the whole colony of hibernating Problems.

"I knew this place was a dump! You guys been enjoyin' yourselves? Seein' the sights?"

And just then, the floodlight on Frank's charmingly slapdash spacesuit started to flicker, and an avalanche of snarling Problems turned the corner.

"There they are. *Nice and spicy*. Where you goin' now, boys? We're just gettin' started!"

The floodlight flicked back on.

"Oh shit."

He turned like a much younger man, spun like a ballerina, and ran for his life. Instantly, his mental map got all jumbled again, and the frog was nowhere to be found this time. I hear he settled down somewhere in the starboard cortex, had some tadpoles with a lovely old photocopy of Frank's high school diploma.

Vigorous snarls rattled off the walls. Frank cocked the shotgun and spun around, mean-muggin' with the best of 'em.

"Hope you brought your appetites!" Two funnels of fire exploded out of the end of the shotgun, illuminating every inch of the tunnel. Frank was pleased. Petrified — pissing himself at this very moment — but pleased too.

He'd cooked these shells up a few weeks ago after a particularly good raid had landed him a *ridiculously* well-stocked pantry. The previous owner had a fondness for hot sauce that rivaled Frank's fondness for breathing, and he simply didn't have room for all of it on board *The Apollo.* So he got creative, and dipped the ends of a few dozen shells in the eye-watering 'habanero hellstorm' on his way out.

"Damn good thinkin', Captain."

A few of the closer Problems were vaporized entirely, reduced to a pungent mist. Others bled battery acid and melted into the walls. Frank wasted no time, turning to run again while he reloaded. "Wish it didn't taste so good."

Between lunches, snacks, dinners, and leftovers, Frank had eaten most of the artillery-grade hot sauce already. As he whirled around to do battle once again, he wondered how his intestines were doing. Maybe he should talk to Duncan, get into baking instead.

"Four down, eight shots left. Gotta start makin' these pouches bigger. I know, I know, bigger the pouch, more fabric you need."

BLAM! BLAM!

"Not to mention thread. Tried to make my own, remember that? Disaster. You try findin' a bobbin anywhere south of Neptune these days." He shook his head ruefully, enjoying the furious screams of the oncoming Problems. "Hard enough gettin' a hold of *yarn,* never mind — "

BLAM! BLAM!

Four shots left now, and in his haste, our intrepid Captain Frank — whose full name, *by the way,* not sure how this hasn't come up yet but I suppose these things happen — his full name is Frank *Mustard.* Guess he doesn't like to talk about it. Would you?

Anyway, in his haste, Frank took a wrong turn. Instead of working his way back to the curious manhole cover that began this whole sorry business, he was suddenly sprinting deeper into the labyrinth, straight into the heart of the Problem — you know, I was going to say 'the Problem's nest,' but let's embrace the happy accident and pretend that was the plan all along.

Frank realized something was amiss when he stepped in a pile of his own fingernails. He tripped, flailed piteously, and landed face to face with his own face. It was a sickly sort of green, but it was also unmistakably *him,* maybe ten years younger? He scrabbled to his feet and looked for a corner to back into, but they were all *occupied.*

Spare parts littered the cave — all the limbs you could ever want, a few that he'd never seen from such unflattering angles, and dozens of half-formed, rotten and abandoned masks of his own *surprised* face. Everything was sprouting out of Problem goo. The whole place was glazed with it, in colors he'd never seen before, anywhere.

"The tumor, and me. We — "

He fired off two of his last rounds into the tidal wave racing down the nearest tunnel towards him. "We grow each other. Left alone, we can't help it. He's part of me." The edge had fallen from Frank's voice. He sounded numb, and deathly tired. "They're all just — parts of me."

He reached up and removed the bandana tied tight around his head. Layer by layer, a dent emerged. A divot, deep in his head, where one of the very first tumors had grown. Nothing grew there now. Not hair, not scar tissue, not so much as a freckle.

The Problems were still scurgling wildly, but there was a new *texture* creeping into the noise. It wasn't just screaming or gurgling anymore, he almost thought he could hear *words* bubbling up underneath it all.

Frank loaded in the last two hot sauce shells and turned to face the horde. They tumbled over each other, fusing and splitting apart again in a sickening electrical storm of hunger and hate.

He held the gun to his chin and smirked. They would not see him panic, not now. The Problems were just yards away, eyes wide with — what was that? Disbelief? Ecstasy? Fear? Frank smirked again, for real this time, and pulled the trigger.

On the other side of the moon, another shot rang out, and another 'Captain' took drastic measures to solve a Problem. Oh, would you look at that? Another fun little coincidence, *or was it?*

"Not good! Not good, not nice, not smart. Stupid Duncan! What were you thinking?" He wasn't thinking. In fact, when the trigger was pulled, he'd been talking. Gave it another go scolding the Problems in the jars, cursing them for — well, here. He was on quite a roll, I'll let him do the honors.

"So now I've got no ship, no crew, no friends, *no purpose* — I'm just shut up in here with a crazy old loon that I admire but *apparently* can't trust even though there's nowhere else to go and no one else to talk to! How am I supposed to go rescue him now and just pretend everything is hunky dory?"

He threw his arms open wide in mock delight. "*Hi honey, how was your day? Build any more neurotic trauma closets? I picked up some vinegar on the way home, I know you need some more so you can jar and pickle your enemies!*"

Duncan tried to catch his breath, only to gasp dramatically when his eyes settled on one of the pickle jarred Problems. "Did you just — *how dare you* roll your eyes at me! I could knock you right off that shelf, watch you cut yourself to ribbons on all that glass! But here I am reaching out for a moment of contact and communication — reaching across enemy lines in a gesture of — *you put those teeth away, right now!*" He pointed to the Problem, and then back at himself. His whole body was trembling. "Here I am, trying to, trying to — what the fuck am I doing?"

And that was when he pulled out the shotgun and completely forgot about Frank's heat ray advice. Caught up in the — well, the moment — he blasted the Problem at point blank range.

BLAM!

Glass everywhere. Vinegar on the ceiling. Problem guts and wood splinters clogging up the air. And somewhere deep inside this maelstrom, an emotionally overwrought *former* Captain realizing that he's just made a not insignificant mistake.

In a flash, he locked the whole room down — closing the air conditioning vents and, for some reason, pulling the shades. Then he locked the door, jiggled the handle just to make sure, released a *jagged* breath, and marched back to the cockpit with a painfully forced grin on his face. "Where were we?"

One of the navigation systems was beeping, and Duncan dove at the distraction. He had programmed the whole scanning apparatus in the ship's mainframe computer to search for signs of organic life. *Any* signs. This beep could only be good news.

"Oh shit."

Dozens of hits had come in. Every new beep was a new *specimen* logged in the database. Duncan scrolled through them and felt that classic sinking feeling in his gut.

"Skeletons. Picked clean, all of them. Piles of bones scattered across the surface, like some sort of — *astronauts, of course!* But natural causes don't break your teeth. Look at that tibia, all scraped up and down. Like they went back for seconds. Marrow, sinew, plasma — midnight snacks."

He furrowed his brows and kept reading. Most of these bones were decades old, but back on *The Clunker,* when the Problem had attacked — just *one* of them, never forget — it had eaten the bones.

Every time he blinked, Duncan saw his First Mate's skull rapidly deteriorating inside the Problem's mangled jaw. The skin had just sloughed off. Lips cratering, cheeks caving in, eyes popping in slow, suspended animation. A cloud of red, eagerly sucked down by the Problem. Gnashing teeth, a filthy belch, and then those frenzied eyes darting around again, searching for the next course. That same eye, later, glued to the oven door, still — hunting.

"Frank?"

A new organic life form had just popped onto the screen, and it looked very much like the Captain of *The Apollo*, his face contorted by terror, blurry, moving at high speed. Duncan whirled around and grabbed the cannon periscope. Frank was moving so fast, it was hard to keep him in focus. And every time he escaped, Duncan's whole field of vision was overrun by a frenzy of Problems.

"Oh good thinking, bring 'em all back here!" Duncan slapped the periscope on his way back to the nav computer. He charted a quick course for the moon's outer orbit and turned on the cannons. This was gonna be tight, but they *might* make it out. If he overclocked the cannons before firing them, the extra heat generation might be enough to take out the Problems. Even if it didn't kill them, it would slow them down. That might be enough.

Duncan ran past the armory and had to double back. His mind was working overtime, faster than he could think. He grabbed the biggest gun he could find and continued on to the visitor's entrance. Frank had said it was jammed before, when Duncan was stranded in open space and desperate for help, but now that he stood before it, everything seemed to be working fine.

"There goes our meet cute." He cocked his head to the side and frowned. "Don't feel so bad about the trophy room now!" He punched a button to open the door and nothing happened. Again, two more times — still nothing. And then a short lever popped out of an unseen compartment.

"*A hand crank?* For a door? That's gonna take forever!" He set down the massive gun and got to work, and it was only halfway through that Duncan realized he was smiling. *The Apollo* wasn't so bad.

A far-off snurgle interrupted his melancholy. "Good point. Gotta stay focused." Duncan felt the door hit the surface, scraping another ugly scrape into the ugly old moon. But before he could raise his eyes to clock Frank's location and make preparations, Frank had arrived, tackling him and screaming for him to close the door again.

Duncan tried and failed to stand up. "Oof!" His voice was a husky squeal, very embarrassing. "You — *knocked the wind out of me.*"

Frank didn't seem to notice. His eyes were wild. "Where's the lever? Come on, kid, fast!"

Duncan wheezed emphatically. "I dropped it when you — *gah, how are you so dense?*"

"The winch, the winch! They were right on my tail!"

Duncan fought to stand, but couldn't manage more than a kneel.

"It's in your hand! Snap out of it, Dunko, this is serious!" He bent down and offered the younger Captain a hand.

Duncan waved him off and attempted to snort. "I'm good here, thanks."

"Suit yourself." Frank grabbed the lever, held the base tight in place against the door hinge, and spun the handle. In a two-second blur, the door was shut tight. Duncan could have killed him then and there.

Frank clapped his hands. "Time's wastin' — we gotta chart a course off this rock, quick as a jackrabbit!" He spun around, and Duncan recognized the shift into 'Captain Mode.' Frank glanced down at him and smirked. "I'm in the chair, so you grab the guns. We'll stand a better chance with a dedicated gunner. Drop the power reserves, redirect it all to the engines til we hit low orbit."

He was interrupted by the roar of the engines, as *The Apollo* took flight. And now it was Duncan's turn to smirk. "I took care of it." The husky squeal was getting worse, almost reaching a supersonic pitch. There were tears in Duncan's bloodshot eyes as he reached for that old bravado. "Not my first time on a ship."

Frank grabbed his arm and pulled him to his feet. "Much obliged."

Duncan choked down a ragged breath and forced his voice down a few octaves. "How was — I mean, what'd you find out there?

Frank laughed bitterly and pulled his bandana out of his back pocket. "Nothin' promisin', lots to — lots to think about." He looked up at Duncan, pulling the bandana taut in his hands.

"You alright, Frank?" For the first time, Duncan noticed the faint scarring across Frank's head, the souvenirs of what looked like hurried, messy surgeries.

"I'm just fine, Duncan, why wouldn't I be?" He took a step closer. "But you knew that already, didn't ya?"

One last wheeze escaped Duncan. He tried to cover it with a cough. "Don't know what you're talking about. Help me get to — the cannons. You drive, and I'll — "

Frank cut him off. "You knew all about me. Knew where to find me." He scoffed, gesturing at *The Apollo*. "Got to know my ship pretty quick too. A whole galaxy out there, and you bump into *me,* trailing an army of Creatures behind you. Funny coincidence."

Duncan backed up, and bumped into a table, inadvertently knocking over a small glass bottle full of orange liquid. "Sorry, I didn't — "

Frank's eyes narrowed. "*If you knew how much I loved that hot sauce* — no more distractions." He took a step closer. "Where did you come from? Who sent you after me?"

Duncan threw up his hands. "Fine! Yes, Frank, I've seen the 'Creatures' before. One of them took down my ship, destroyed everything I have and everyone I — "

Frank leaned in so close that Duncan could see his veins pop one by one. "I told you what would happen if you lied to me about this, didn't I?"

"*Yes* — but that doesn't give you the right to *kill* me!" Duncan spluttered guiltily, searching for the right words. "I was scared, and alone! You don't understand!"

The older Captain guffawed cruelly. "*I don't understand? I've been out here for YEARS, by myself* — "

Duncan backpedaled, quickly changing the subject with a sudden, forced nonchalance. "And so what, I got mad and fired off a few rounds, broke a few jars? After what they did to me, it's the least they deserve!"

Frank recoiled in a wild panic, but Duncan was on a roll now. "And yes, I might have lost track of the Problem on the space oven, but that's *my* problem, not yours! Not *my* — *you know what I mean!*" A fresh wave of wheezing almost drove him to his knees. "Just let me — just let me catch my breath here and I'll take care of 'em both."

Frank's hand flew to his hip. "*Both?* You set two of them loose on my ship?"

"Well, no. The first one, the eyeball — he could be anywhere." Frank drew his gun, but Duncan didn't seem to notice. "And the second one, I locked him in — *I locked him in your secret lair!*"

Frank tried to keep his voice calm. "One more time, Dunko. I'm askin' you one more time. Who sent you here to kill me?"

Duncan blanched. His mouth actually fell open. "That's — *kill you?* Frank, I'm trying to save your life here!"

Frank squeezed his eyes shut and shook his head. "Was it the army? *The Clunker,* were you runnin' ops for the army in that thing? Is that it, they made you Captain on the condition you finally brought me in?"

"You're talking nonsense!" Duncan took a cautious step closer. "*The Clunker* was a shipping vessel. I was trying to buy it out from a trading company before the *Problem* — I was a glorified mailman, Frank! Just a cargo captain stranded in open space, begging for his life!"

Frank dropped the shotgun on the counter. His nostrils burned from the last of the hot sauce floating in the air.

"I'm handcuffin' you in the gunnery nest. You're gonna look out for 'Problems' while I clean up your mess." He took a deep breath. "And when I'm done, I'm throwin' you off my ship. No escape pods, I'm afraid, but maybe you can have my space oven. *Should feel right at home!*"

Dread is a funny feeling. Funny like nervous laughter, it's an involuntary response. Some people laugh when they get hit. Some people feel dread when their life starts going too well. But only a select few brain-broken whackadoos react to certain, impending doom by uncontrollably *smiling*.

"Woah, what's all that about? Cut that out." Frank grimaced at Duncan's sudden, dazzling smile.

"Sorry, it's a panic thing. Hasn't happened for a long time."

"Well put a lid on it, would ya?" Frank gestured vaguely at Duncan's entire being. "Or blink, somethin'. You're freakin' me out."

Duncan did his very best to blink, but it came out more like a wince. "Yeah, I'm trying. Talk about something else, maybe that'll help."

Frank rolled his eyes and mopped up the last of the hot sauce. "Think of England, you sonofabitch bastard. I don't care how happy you are about it, the second we're done here, you're walkin' the plank."

"That's not helping, *that's not helping.* My face hurts, I think I pulled something — "

Frank cut him off with an exaggerated scoff. "Oh, you tried to, that's for *damn* sure."

Duncan whirled around and actually stomped his foot — still smiling frantically. "*WHY* do you talk like that? You tell me you're this haunted old astronaut but you talk like some frontiersman good ole boy. I don't buy it, I don't like it, and — *and I'm sick of it!*"

"Well now, that's an interesting story, if you're really wantin' to hear it." Frank scoffed again, more gently this time, and sauntered over to the nav computer.

Duncan shrugged. "Yeah, sure, that sounds great. Whatever you got, hit me."

Frank punched in a few commands and shook his head. "You hear them 'Problems' outside before takeoff? Howlin' at the moon, bayin' like wild hogs."

"Yes, Frank, I heard them. I think I still do, maybe we should — "

"Oh, so it's 'we' now!"

Duncan could've sworn he heard one of his teeth crack. "What do you want from me? Should I toss myself out into space? Shove my head in the engine block?" His smile widened. "Do you actually want me to be your latrine cadet? I have no shame, I have no pride, I have nothing left to give you!"

A blood vessel burst in Duncan's left eye as he started spiraling. "Where is it? Where is this almighty space toilet? Point me in the right direction, my noble Captain Cowboy Howdy Doody Spaceman! I'll lick it clean, you just wait!"

Frank pushed back from the console. "Nobody's lickin' toilets on my ship. Not now, not ever." He stood up, and tried to suppress a sudden twang of sympathy. "Your Problems are my problems now, but that don't make us a 'we' — ain't no teamwork with liars. Not possible. Now if you'll calm down long enough to listen, it's taken care of."

He extended one finger and dramatically pressed the big red 'Enter' button. A tinny, flat computer voice blared out from the console. "INITIATE SELF-*DEFENSE* PROCEDURES."

Frank straightened his spacesuit. "As for your original question – "

"About your accent?"

"No, not that one." Frank sighed as the twang of sympathy faded away. "The other question. What I 'want' from you. And I'll tell ya." He smiled, and let the moment hang between them. "But we gotta go kill this thing while we have our little chat. Come on now." He led Duncan past the gun turret, which was lazily flopping back and forth. Nothing was creaking, but something was definitely broken. "Auto-pilot for the guns — not great — so let's be quick about this. You last saw it in my study, is that right?"

"Oh yes, *glooping* down the side of a lunatic's pickle jar."

"Easy, Dunko. And I told you before, I'm gonna need you to start blinkin' real soon — or I'm gonna have to put ya down."

Duncan's smile blazed back to life. "Old faithful! The solution to every problem. Why not? Just keep killing everything in the universe, great plan!"

"Were you *plannin'* to cohabitate with these monsters? That why you set one of 'em free on my ship?" Frank whirled around. "When we find it, maybe you two can go play fetch outside!"

"*How dare you!* I'm the one who shot it, aren't I?"

Frank spoke through gritted teeth. "You *can't* shoot them, Duncan. Not with a shotgun, anyway. Just makes 'em angrier, splits 'em. Multiplies the issue!" He flapped his arms indignantly. "*You don't think I tried shootin' them?*"

"I wouldn't know, you don't tell me anything! For example, when exactly did you go from trying to *kill* them to collecting them?"

Frank spun around and punched the wall. Duncan's strained, crusty eyes jumped at the sound, and he suddenly noticed a great number of other dents marking the walls of *The Apollo*.

"Life is a two-sided coin." Frank massaged his hand while he spoke. "You got your fuck-ups, and your recalibrations. If you're lucky, you land on recalibration the first time." He turned over the injured hand. "But if not, you just gotta keep flippin' the coin! And sometimes you don't immediately know which is which."

He scrunched up his face, looking for the perfect words. "It's like a metaphor. One side of the coin, nice milk chocolate. On the other side, a nice milky shit. But how do you not know all of this already, O *Captain?*"

Duncan took a moment to — process. "That's the difference between you and me." His voice was calm, but cutting. "*I* confided in my crew. I trusted my crew, looked out for them. Hell, I actually *had* a crew, and I armed them with the information they needed — instead of sending them off to die with a weapon I knew was useless against the enemy."

Frank's face lit up innocently. "Hey, that all sounds great to me. *How's it workin' out for* 'em?"

Duncan gasped, and the rage that flooded through him burned right through the anxiety.

His lockjaw smile melted away. "That's a really great question, Frank. How many years have you spent hunting Problems again? How many hair dryers and pickle jars have you taken off the streets in that time? Would you say the universe is safer now than it was when you started?"

He smacked his own head and leaned in. "Or maybe — just maybe — could it be that your failure to kill these 'Creatures' *or* tell the rest of us about them makes you responsible for the death of my crew, and who knows how many other people over the years?"

Now it was Frank's turn to gasp. He backed away from Duncan and bumped into the door frame, but his thoughts went further back, drifting through time like a lily pad down a lazy river.

"CONFIRMED,   CAPTAIN.   REROUTING NAVIGATION SYSTEMS. EVASIVE MANEUVERS ACTIVE."

The dry, humorless computer voice echoed down through the years. He was pacing in front of the cockpit. *The Apollo* was rattling along through some heavy turbulence. Frank couldn't place the memory exactly. It was recent, he thought, but he'd been out here so long now. It was getting harder to pin anything down.

"An asteroid field, out of nowhere, two days after hitting the last belt. Picked up by *none* of the computers. Failure on every level.

Structural damage to the hull, *another antenna gone*, and for what?"

He heard his own voice like it was a stranger's, but the details were settling in now. A food transport had imploded outside Saturn, must've been six months ago. No survivors, barely any food, but it had a drive-thru window — he remembered that part. Lotta finicky little pastries. Those stale pastel burgers, brownies on popsicle sticks.

"ORGANIC LIFE FORMS DETECTED. HOSTILE. COMPOSITION UNKNOWN."

Frank watched himself launch into action. He was strapped into the gunnery booth in an instant, scanning the horizon for threats. Monsters and ghosts.

"Computer, run a scan for my DNA. Isolate the results and redirect engine power to the cannons."

A glass panel emerged from the wall, lined with a complex matrix of reference points and munition metrics. His field of vision turned green, and then certain asteroids started to light up. The guns roared to life in his hands.

"Trace their heat signatures, as far back as possible. To the source."

The targets were down in ten seconds. He watched himself work, helplessly. The overlay panel retracted, and he saw his own face squint out into the darkness.

"Analogue scan, just to make sure. *Where are you?*"

The first Creature made contact, slamming against the cockpit windshield. It was sliding towards him, scraping deep gouges in the glass with its teeth. He could see pastry and bits of pilot in its belly.

"Yeah, I fuckin' thought so. Ships don't implode anymore. Too many failsafes. Computer, scan the ship's exterior, then open exhaust chambers. *All of* 'em. Vent all available heat."

This was an old trick, but it worked every time. Dump the heat, shake 'em off, then blast 'em.

"RESULTS GATHERED, HEAT SIGNATURE TRACKING SUCCESSFUL."

An asteroid collision rocked *The Apollo.* Frank watched himself brace for another impact, gritting his teeth and squeezing his eyes shut. The ship sounded bad. Nuts and bolts, that's all this thing was, and it could rattle apart to nothing in minutes. He was always just minutes away.

"Computer, read out results."

"IN REVERSE CHRONOLOGICAL ORDER, SATURN, MARS, DELTA CENTAURI — "

"Damnit, I know all of those. Cleared 'em out a dozen times over. Scraped the surface, scanned every stone. *You* told me they were clear! Go back further."

The exhaust vents twisted and squealed open. He heard them, he *felt* them belching white hot flames. Creatures melted off the side of *The Apollo,* and he blew them apart before they could recover.

"Computer, send full power to the engines. Reverse sixty-five degrees, secondary thrusters. Line up primary thrusters with the debris, then hit the throttle. Overclock the engine room, Authorization 74275. *Burn* 'em *out.*"

He heard himself muttering, not to the computer anymore, not to posterity or memory. Not to anyone, but Frank knew what he was saying. Four Creatures, that's all he'd taken out that day, and no new leads from the scan. He'd been everywhere by now, twice, but who was to say the computer knew jack shit? *He knew.* They had gone to ground. The Creatures were hiding, just like he was. They both knew the rules. He wasn't a hunter, he was an exterminator.

"Need the source! The nest. Their home base."

But he knew their source, didn't he? He'd always known the creature's *point of origin.* Even the rickety-ass, no-good computer knew, but he had interrupted it before the readout could get that far. Didn't need to hear it again. He knew in every moment of every day, he knew every time he saw one and felt that same thousand-pound stabbing pain in his chest. That look of recognition in their hateful eyes.

"Hundreds, thousands of raids. They always come back. None for months, a flash of hope, and then — you find a new colony. Festering, frothing — feeding."

The engines kicked and rumbled behind him, but after a second or two they caught, and he felt the Creatures die, torn apart in a rush of hellfire. The feeling brought him no comfort.

"Frank? Frank, come on — wake up!" There was a voice shouting *directly* into his ear. "Damnit, you hit your head, let me get this headband off."

Frank grumbled back to life. "No! Get off me. Just — give me space." *The Apollo* came back into focus, and then he saw Duncan — and scowled. "Help me up already, you sorry sack of shit. Unless you wanna keep shoutin' at me instead. Just get me a pillow, I'll catch up on my beauty rest. Heh."

Duncan grabbed his hand and pulled Frank to his feet. Awkwardly, he dusted off the older man's shoulder. "Sorry about what I said."

Frank didn't meet his eye. "We got a job to do, Dunko. Quit yer cryin'." He started marching towards his study, but two steps down the hallway, he had to grab the wall for support.

"I shouldn't have said that about yer crew." And then he was gone, huffing and puffing through the ship.

Duncan followed him. "Like I — uh, said before, I tried to seal up your — the *room* behind me."

"Not so easy to kill, these Problems. Ya did the right thing."

Duncan withdrew the shotgun Frank had given him on the moon. It was shockingly heavy in his hands, but stable too. "Trade ya for the heat ray."

Frank smiled. "Look at you, gettin' the lay of the land. Deal." They swapped weapons, and he gave Duncan a quick, down and dirty tutorial. This was going to be much easier with two people. "If they're too big, they'll fight back. Might just absorb the heat, like you're sittin' 'em by the fire and pourin' some cocoa." He shook his head like a dusty snow-globe. "But if I hit 'em with a few slugs first, cut the fuckers down to size, then you can burn 'em down to nothin'."

Duncan was impressed. "Like those little marshmallows."

"Exactly. Wasn't sure you'd get that reference. How old are ya anyway?"

"I got to spend a few good years on the surface before evac." Duncan tried to smile. "A few real good years."

"That's great to hear. Can't imagine growing' up in some colony, learnin' to ride a bike on a space station!"

Duncan's face fell, and he remembered that the space oven was gone. "I did some of that too, and you're right. No fun at all."

Frank tested the door gingerly. "You alright, kid?"

"Oh yeah, all good."

"Gotta be ready with the heat ray, all I'm sayin'."

Duncan bristled. "Don't you worry about me. Just focus on the sawed-off. Shot, chaser."

"Good man." Frank squinted his left eye and took aim. "Guns up, Dunko. On my mark." Frank felt for the sweet spot under the hinge and smiled. It was an involuntary thing. And with the agility of a much younger man, he dug his boot into the scrap metal of the office door. It exploded open, crumpling under the pressure — and they were in.

BLAM! BLAM! Bzzzt. Bzzzt. Kekeke. Bzzzt.

Duncan staggered back. "Damn, you weren't kiddin'." It happened faster than he would've believed possible. A flurry of movement, flashes of green, his body fighting to recoil, to run. And then two blasts from the shotgun, and he was squeezing the trigger on the heat ray.

They writhed and melted. One of 'em might have popped. A rush of acid green, blazing bright and angry, almost turning a sickly sort of yellow, and then burning — from the inside out — screeching so loud his hair stood on end.

Frank slid the shotgun back into his suit. "Never gets any easier. You alright?"

"I'm fine. Felt good, actually. Did we get 'em all?"

Frank laughed, but it wasn't a mocking sound. To Duncan, it sounded like a dog dying. "That's the trick, ain't it? You never get 'em all. What'd you say before — shot, chaser."

Duncan barely heard Frank's response. He was tracking the green goo up the wall, past the air conditioning vent he had hurriedly slammed shut. But the trail went cold just past the vent. Two green dribbles clung to the scuffed up shell of an exposed electrical socket.

"Would that have killed it, climbing in there?"

Frank's hand absently moved to his chest. He tried to pass it off as a scratch. "Afraid not, but it might turn orange. Listen for the crackle."

He started quickly barking out orders to the ship computer, but Duncan's eyes had returned to the smoldering bodies of the Problems they *had* managed to kill. The last vestiges of boiling yellow plasma were curdling into mist and disappearing. When was the last time he ate something? He couldn't remember. Might've been on *The Clunker*, before his incarceration. Why was he even thinking about this? The sight of three cremated Problems was hardly appetizing.

Duncan responded, but he was on auto-pilot now. "Sounds good. I'm right behind you." It was Frank's comment about growing up on a space station. He had stirred it all up again. Talking about evac, his childhood, the space oven. That perfect shade of yellow.

Frank's voice was a distant growl. "Alright, that gives us a lead. The mainframe has collapsed, everything but the lights and the guns. Hope you didn't have anywhere to be, looks like the engines are out for the time bein'."

"So we're headed to the engine room? Fix it up?"

Frank was laser focused. "Headed that way, yeah. Lookin' for tracks along the way. Clues."

Duncan trailed behind him, but his body was fully on auto-pilot. *The Apollo* was floating away from him, like dust off a chalkboard. He had been in school. Home economics, if he wasn't mistaken. Call from his mother, she was on her way to pick him up. He had argued, didn't want to leave. The teacher was teasing some can't-miss oatmeal recipes. *The perfect start to your day, using ingredients you already had in your pantry!* He'd been transfixed, bedazzled. Truth be told, it was his only good subject.

Frank's voice drifted back to him. "It's all about knowing' what to look for. A disturbance, debris, *somethin'* that just ain't right."

His mother had been crying when the car pulled up. There had been an accident at work, she'd only just heard herself. His father was dead.

"Gah! There go the lights. Hold on a second, I've got a light here somewhere. Chewin' wires, the stupid prick. We'll show 'im, don't you worry."

He had heard somewhere that these things always happened in pairs. They hadn't even held a funeral yet, hadn't even called the caterer. Another call, from the next door neighbor. *Turn on the tv, any channel.* Was this real? The neighbors couldn't believe it, none of his friends could believe it either. But it made perfect sense to Duncan and his mother. Of course the world was ending.

"There you go, hold that. Careful with the spittin' end. That there's a flare, one of my very last ones. Look at you, flare in one hand, heat ray in the other, like a real spaceman. The trick now, the whole ballgame, is to move slow. Slow and careful."

Apparently, some missile test had gone wrong, and punched a hole in some environmental something, upset the balance of something else, and now the climate was going to turn, rapidly. He didn't really understand. He was ten. His mom had told him it was like a balloon, and all the air was going to leak out of the atmosphere. Planetary evacuations had been ordered, his Dad's job had made arrangements for them. The traffic, the sirens, hurried introductions and long goodbyes. He remembered asking if everyone was going to make it out in time, if he would have to miss more school.

"You see that, Dunko? Goin' round the corner. Sheepshit, it was there a second ago."

They settled on a small station outside Ganymede. A couple days in, he started doing the math. There were forty people onboard, and only a few hundred stations up and running. News reports said Earth had descended back into an ice age, that it was uninhabitable. His mother stopped talking about a funeral. But a few days later, she brought him something.

"Look at that, here — hold the flare closer to the ground. See that? Tracks. We smoked him out. Stay sharp now. He's close."

Duncan realized then, for the first time, that they were gone. Not just his parents, but his father's stripes, which he had kept in his nightstand for more than twenty years. They must have blown up with *The Clunker* — or rather, burned up when *he* had hit the self-destruct on *The Clunker*.

Guilt coursed through him like bacon grease in a septic system. He'd made a promise to those stripes, to his Dad, that he would make him proud. Whatever that meant. That he would be his own man, and one day, maybe even — a Captain.

BLAM! BLAM! Bzzzt. Bzzzt.

"Missed him. No — wait — we tagged him! See that drip? That's you, kid. Means we both made contact. Now, we just passed the engine room. Still dead. Only potential targets left down this way — aw, hell."

Duncan came back to himself. "What is it? Where's it hiding?"

Frank looked uncharacteristically *uncomfortable*. "To tell ya the truth, the ship's a little backloaded. Usually ya get hit from the front — asteroids, enemy fire — so I threw a lot of the more vulnerable shit back here. Sorta piled up."

"Answer me, Frank. Where is it hiding?"

"I don't know! Could be the furnace, the backup generator room, the munitions depot, or — or the escape pod. *Always hated those things. Turned it into more of a storage unit, really.*"

Duncan braced himself. "For what?"

"Dynamite." Frank took a sudden interest in the burned patch of his spacesuit, avoiding eye contact. "Scavenged a whole palette, few years back."

"Well that rules out the heat ray, and the shotgun too."

Frank looked up, struck by sudden inspiration. "Unless we chase him back out to the ship proper."

"*Chase* him? We're not catchin' mice here, Frank."

Frank brushed him off. "Oh, I do it all the time." He quickly unspooled his injured arm and winked at Duncan. Then he tore open the wound and cocked the shotgun. The Problem came out of nowhere, like a neon cannonball, drooling and chomping its awful little teeth.

BLAM! Bzzzt. BLAM! Bzzzt. Bzzzt.

Duncan squinted into the shadows. Frank punched the wall again and started to reload. "Missed him again. Guns up!"

"Frank — watch your six!"

Frank patted down his suit. "I'm outta shells, kid."

Duncan swung the sawed-off like a baseball bat, screaming like a wild man — and I'll be damned if it didn't just work. On a regulation field, the hit would've easily been a double. But Duncan went for MVP, ripping off his helmet in a moment of divine inspiration. He'd read about it once, as a kid, baseball players throwing their gloves to catch the ball, and then just catching the glove.

"Run, kid, the engine room!" Frank fired off a quick command to the ship computer and the lights crackled back on. The Problem hissed at the cheap halogens. Duncan tried his very best not to make eye contact with — it — but he tripped on a floor cable.

"Fuckin' goddamn piece of shit!"

He had *just* enough time to give the helmet some topspin before it flew out of his hands, caught the Problem — and sailed directly into the newly reawakened furnace. The Problem erupted, splattering onto the helmet visor and collapsing into the flames.

"That's what I'm talkin' about, Dunko! Great save — the footwork, the sheer fuckin' piss and vinegar of it! You hear that sizzle? That's all you! Got a goddamn grill-master on my ship!"

Frank slapped him on the back and went in for a handshake, but Duncan was staring out the window. Out the crummy old porthole window that Frank had installed back here on an errant whim. "No. Not real. It's just a memory. *A memory.*"

Frank followed Duncan's gaze. A shaky, shoestring abomination was shambling towards them. Rusted, twisted up ship parts, glued back together by the only glue in the universe that had teeth. Frank had never seen so many Problems in one place.

"No — *Duncan, is that* — "

Duncan's voice was hollow. His mind was frozen.

"*The Clunker.*"

Chapter Seven: <u>Dogfight</u>

It's tough, being a middle child. Even worse if you're an underachiever, and a screw-up. Worse still if one of your parents is extraordinarily successful and overbearing. The pressure and expectations of such a life, the endless comparisons — it's enough to drive anyone a little wacky. You see your brothers rising through the ranks, really *making something of themselves,* and there you are — a dud. An afterthought. An embarrassment, tucked away in the back of family photos.

Resentment festers within you. Old grudges harden. You shut out the world and spurn the very concept of self-improvement. A vicious cycle develops. You hate the world, you hate yourself, you hate everything and everyone. And then you start to lash out. You seethe and plot, you sabotage and scheme.

Eventually, you overreach. You try something too big, too vindictive — and then they're all watching. You can't hide anymore, but it's too late to backpedal. You're committed. And if the plan doesn't work, you're screwed. It's your last shot, your only chance,

the grand finale of your entire miserable life.
It all comes down to one fateful day.

And here we reach a crossroads. The being to which I keep hypothetically referring is quite literally a Problem. And he is somewhat distinct from the other Problems we have encountered — a different beast than the one that Duncan just threw into a furnace, the original 'Creature' that grew in Frank's chest, any of the gloopy murderers that *recolonized* the moon, or even that big Problem who ate Jupiter. No, this particular Problem is his own Problem. He's an individual, a uniquely cancerous blight on the solar system with his very own thoughts and feelings.

He has a special part to play in this story, and because of that, I'm afraid that we will have to give him a name. Nothing too fancy, he's still a fucking tumor, but we need *some* way to differentiate him from the countless, nameless masses. 'Prob' is a natural choice, a dispassionate abbreviation of the original *'Problem'* — it's decidedly *not* a nickname, but neither is it fun to say.

'Rob' is right there too, I suppose, or maybe 'Robert' if we want to preserve that whiff of disapproval. Might be too humanizing though, next to 'Frank' and 'Duncan' — don't want to put them on equal footing. We could go darker and more literal, call him 'Frankie' or

'Junior,' but those both feel too familiar. Let's go back to the drawing board. *Problem.* Rob. Probby. Blem. *Bleh.*

Lem — now that's something. Ooh, how about Lemmy? It's slippery, slimy. There's an ugliness to the name, the way you have to stick your tongue out a little and press it into your teeth. It's not fun. Your tongue resents it. You can't trust a 'Lemmy,' can you? Of course not. *Lemmy*, that's it. Let's go with Lemmy, and if it doesn't work out, we can revisit the others.

Lemmy's big day, when it did finally arrive, started off pretty well. He snagged a light breakfast on the way in — a brightly-colored ambulance ship that didn't even have a weapons system. He almost felt bad. *Almost.* But if a fish is stupid enough to get in the barrel full of bullet holes, then he deserves what he gets. And besides, Lemmy was hungry. He needed a clear mind to pull off this spectacle. And make no mistake, that's exactly what this was.

Lemmy finished digesting the last few EMTs, took a few deep, shuddering, grotesque breaths, and sent out the signal. It was a lot like having a thought, if you could focus all the electricity in your brain into one nasty, hateful surge, squeeze your eyes shut so hard that you shit yourself, and then release all that energy in one tectonic blast.

Every Problem within a hundred lightyears rattled in place as the message went out. Their horrible little teeth ground against each other, paradoxically and unfortunately *sharpening* as their minds drifted to pick up Lemmy's formal invitation. He could feel the ping zooming out in all directions, and almost immediately, the answering growls came lumbering back through limitless spacetime. The audience were beginning to take their seats. It was almost showtime.

Of course, you already know how Lemmy's big spectacle flamed out. Most of the galaxy's remaining Problems were there, waiting and watching for days on end, as Lemmy *failed* to pull off his daring one-man siege of *The Clunker*. Tens of thousands of Problems bore witness to his shame, chortling hideously as he rocketed around the ship, hunting endlessly for the last living crew member — that rambling dunce on the intercom.

The rest of them died easy, barely putting up a fight, so who was this maddening holdout? By the time they met face to face, as you will no doubt recall, it was far too late. Captain Duncan Arugula had already activated the ship's self-destruct. *The Clunker* exploded in a shimmering fireball of mutual resentment and ineptitude. Duncan sailed away in his beloved space oven, and Lemmy was reduced to an angry smear of what had once been a formidable left eyeball. He was awash in self-loathing, boiling over with rage — and stupid Duncan was right there, just waiting to be blamed for everything.

And then, barely five minutes later, the amateur astronaut threw open the space oven door to talk to some other blasted human — and there went Lemmy, flung suddenly into the outer reaches of the universe. It took him a moment to process what was happening. That other human, he knew him. There was something astonishingly familiar there. Not his voice, not his face. It was deeper than that. He felt a phantom ache, like his teeth were grinding — but that was ridiculous. This was a meaningless human, not another Problem. And besides, he didn't have any teeth anymore, or even a mouth to put them in.

Lemmy spiraled out of sight, slipping beyond the spiteful gaze of his assembled brothers and even — for a few chapters at least — passing under the radar of this very narrative. But he was still there, in the background, nestled deep in the scenery, *watching.* Really though, at this point what else would you expect him to be doing? He's an eyeball, soaring aimlessly through the cosmos — until, that is, he discovered that he *could* 'aim,' somewhat.

His cornea, or iris, whatever the colorful part is called, was now more than a quarter of his entire body mass, and that meant that it had some real sway. If he rolled his eye hard enough, Lemmy discovered that he could just slightly alter his flight trajectory. And that was enough, after a fashion. He spun like a broken compass, drawing energy from who knows where at this point, until he landed on the worthless husk that we call a moon. It was a brand new world for him, dusty and crusty and hopeless, just like his future. But there was an energy here too, a faint but unshakeable familiarity that reminded him strangely of the human.

Lemmy tried his very best to dismiss these impossible thoughts, but it gets harder to control your mind after your brain is blown up and scatted across the Milky Way. And then, just as he was starting to move on and rebuild his life with the other destroyed Problems he found hiding out in the mess of tunnels running through the moon, the human was back. This time, he was armed, but not with the usual, useless shooty shooties.

How did this human know so much about them? Their weaknesses, their hideouts, their — *instincts*. Lemmy watched helplessly as more of his brothers were melted and splattered across the cave walls, until the tide finally began to turn. Quite literally, a writhing horde of Problems descended upon the mysterious hunter. Lemmy was irate. First this stranger robs him of the chance to kill his own brothers *himself* — when they're already injured and vulnerable — and then he gives the rest of them the bragging rights of killing the big bad human invader?

Another feather in everyone else's cap, *but no,* no feathers for ole Lemmy! No cap for Lemmy, no head to put in on, no teeth to defend his honor — nothing. But then, just as Lemmy had given up hope of a freak cave-in that would kill everyone involved in this little charade, the human began to act very strangely. He stopped running, and unwrapped a dirty old bandana from his head. There was a dent in *his* noggin too, but Lemmy was in no mood to *relate* to this despicable creature.

They were enemies, opposites, the bitterest possible rivals. Him and that stupid stowaway Captain had destroyed Lemmy's dreadful life. Everything was worse now. He could never show his face at home again, not after the *Clunker* fiasco. And his brothers, oh his beloved brothers, they would make *telling father* their first priority — maybe even above eating.

Then he would officially be an exile, or they would just kill him. The last thing he would see would be his father's massive teeth collapsing on top of him. Grinding him up into gooey oblivion, and then he would just be one more gloopy glob in the hive. Thrown in with countless others, buried with a million other Problems in his father's belly. Back to whatever had come before, before he'd sprouted his own eyeballs and teeth and broken free. He didn't wanna go back there.

Shock horror broke through the fog of Lemmy's self-pity. The light from that monster's flamethrower had changed, falling momentarily across that sizable divot in his head. The skin was roiling, pumping and pulsating, stretching to its breaking point. Veins popped and blood surged — *and all of it was green*, rising to meet the oncoming Problems. Lemmy could hardly believe his eye. The human was sending out the signal, calling them to him. He felt the pull, they all did, and without even deciding to, he found himself moving closer to the center of the cave, where all the tunnels met.

But then he felt a prickle, all over the skin he didn't have anymore — this was all wrong. There was danger here. He rolled his eye feverishly, shuffling along at a truly pathetic speed, but it was just enough to save him as the tunnels crashed down around him. He saw a flash of the human's gun, a strategically hidden shooty shooty, and then that knowing smile. The creature wasn't afraid to die, and he wanted them to know it. And then he was gone, dodging out of the way of the blast and collapsing the ceiling at its thinnest, weakest point. Lemmy was almost impressed, but he managed to talk himself down to jealous.

The moon crumbled around him. He felt his brothers dying, crushed and pasted and petitely diced by the falling debris — but for whatever reason, Lemmy survived. A colossal weight of rocky ceiling crashed down across from him, and once again, he found himself being flung out into open space. Once again, he cursed the human responsible for his misfortune, but almost immediately, he was interrupted by more signals. Pleas for help, yowls of imminent demise, and underneath it all — always — that growl of hunger.

This would not pass unnoticed, even if his great shame with *The Clunker* raid did. His father would know about this already, and perhaps *already* be on his way to respond. To avenge the dead, to devour their corpses, to consume their malice and add ever more to his own. *Dread* consumed Lemmy once again, and he glanced back at the shrinking moon. The tunnels had caught fire, and the fire had spread. It looked like a big frowny face staring back at him, with a roaring chasm where the left eyeball should be — perfect.

And that latest, unbearable wave of hatred sparked within Lemmy a new idea, a larger, grander spectacle than anything he'd ever seen attempted. He rolled his eye back frantically, diving into the project with total, gleeful abandon. He had no face left to him, but he still felt a nasty smile curling at his mouth. After all, this *was* still his big day.

Now that we're all on the same page again, let's return to the flight deck of the embattled *Apollo*. Duncan and Frank had both sprung into action at the sight of the zombified *Clunker* lurching towards them. Neither of them had even *begun* to emotionally process what was happening, but there would be time for that later — if they made it to later. Frank had taken charge, breaking into a cold sweat and firing off familiar orders. The computer buzzed and beeped, and Duncan moved to the cockpit in a daze. Frank's voice followed him, corkscrewing into his nerves.

"Good man! I'm giving' you the reigns here, Dunko, so please don't fuck it up!" Frank was already strapping himself into the gunnery booth. Autopilot was't going to cut it anymore, and he knew these cannons better than the manufacturers at this point.

"Hey kid, jump on the comms!"

Duncan clicked the old flight helmet into his suit. His mind dimly observed that he finally had a radio in his suit now, but the joke — if it was a joke — fell flat. He was a million miles and several decades away, reliving every bad memory that the conversation with Frank had resurfaced.

"Copy that, Frank. Quick — uh — quick question for ya."

"This again. Fine. I've been out here a long time, all by my lonesome." He paused for a moment as the guns reached a full charge, screaming into the void — and Duncan's ear piece — as a hundred pounds of boiling point plasma slugs lit up the heavens.

Frank could feel the muscles in his fists tearing, that old sloshing feeling as his brain rocked against his skull. This was what it was all about. He whirled in the booth, turning on a *hay penny*, raining down hellfire on his enemies like a one-man Pompeii.

Frank reached up to loosen his bandana. "Anyway, I was sayin' — ya get bored. Goin' through the ship, catalogin' and reorganizin', inspections and inventories — you know how it is, eventually I find a few movies tucked away. Might've been some peace offering for the aliens, a taste of our great culture. All westerns, obviously."

He snorted, and it sounded like a cannon blast over the radio. "I don't know what to say, Dunko! You spend a few decades out here with nothin' and no one but John Wayne and you'll come out of it a little fucked in the head too. Coulda been worse. That old Hollywood accent, all chippy and nasal-like. Or it coulda been silent movies, turned me into a fuckin' mime!"

Frank quietly realized that this might be a teachable moment for the young Captain. "Tell ya what, we survive this and maybe I'll show ya one. Take your mind off things. *There we go!* Just knocked a wing loose — oh they're scramblin' now, I'll tell ya!" He squinted as the static rolled in through his earpiece. "Dunko? Dunko, you still there?"

He was, technically, still present on the ship.

"Affirmative, Captain. Copy that. One wing down." Duncan shook himself and took control of *The Apollo*, keeping them *within* shooting range but *out* of boarding range. "Frank — you ever see this before?" He sped up, trying to marshal his thoughts. "Is this — normal for Problems? Insult to injury, the chase, the recycling — how many *Apollos* have you gone through over the years?"

He could hear his voice reaching that dangerous, wheezy pitch again, but he couldn't stop himself. "These blood feuds and vendettas — vendetta? Whatever. They never end, and I don't know if I can do this forever. Indefinitely, you know? Haven't slept since — *how do you* — never mind. Uh, ignore me. Hold target on the other wing. I'll keep you in range."

A rush of static came through the radio. It sounded *exactly* like the tv had right before the evac order had come through. Duncan shook himself again as Frank's voice drowned out the static.

"Truth be told, kid, I got no idea. Ya just keep pushin', til you can't push anymore, and then you keep goin'." Frank took his time, measuring every word. "I know this thing only ends one way, but that don't mean I'm gonna roll over. Don't know how."

"How long have you been doing this? Since evac? But when did the Problems show up?" Duncan's eyes lost focus. "And you've known about them forever, from what you've said." He was tripping over his own thoughts, trying to put it all together, trying desperately to stay in the present moment without thinking about what was presently happening.

Frank frowned at the stars. "Well, to your previous question, this is my one and only *Apollo.* Found that numberin' 'em just makes you sad. None of that Thomas Edison lightbulb bullshit. Doesn't happen, just makes you feel like a screw-up. As for huntin' creatures, well — that's been goin' on a long time. Before your *evacuation*, back before all these colonies too. Scattered militaries. Pirates. Wasn't always such a mess, I can tell ya that much."

The targeting computer started screaming, and Duncan switched off his radio to spare Frank's ears.

"ERROR. INCOMING DATA. HOSTILE SHIP CONTAINS UNKNOWN LIFEFORMS. MUNITIONS SCAN COMPLETE. PROJECTILES CONFIRMED, CONTACT IMMINENT. ERROR."

"Hey, easy there. Down, boy. Girl? I dunno." Duncan patted the computer gently. "C'mon, what's wrong? What's the error?"

"DATA REPORTS CONFIRM PROJECTILES *CONTAIN* UNKNOWN LIFEFORMS. ERROR. REPEAT. DATA REPORTS CONFIRM — "

Duncan finally found the mute button and flipped the radio back on, glancing guiltily back at the flashing screen.

"Frank, you seein' this?"

"*I repeat, comms down, comms down!* Dunko? Shit, you scared me. You okay?"

Duncan glanced back at the computer. "Oh sure. Just trying to work this old ass system you've got here. Projectiles inbound."

"Well, slap my ass and call me a chicken!"

Duncan agreed, though he couldn't recall that particular turn of phrase from John Wayne's filmography. He could see his ship out the porthole window. No, not *his* ship. *The Clunker* was dead. The crew was gone. Their Captain was gone. None of its parts worked anymore. But the Problems that were puppeteering its corpse had found a novel use for the burned-out weapons system. He had to squint to see them, but there they were. His stomach fell through his boots. The computer was right.

"They're shooting Problems at us!"

Hundreds of hungry little bullets were streaming towards *The Apollo*. They were small, insidiously small, much too small to hit with a run-down Triple Watt 95 laser cannon weapons system, but the perfect size to worm inside every crack and open pipe of a spaceship.

"Frank, we have to shut it down. The guns, the engine. We have ten seconds to impact — *if that* — and we have to turn this ship into a fortress, *now!*" He didn't wait for confirmation. Duncan defied his Captain and killed the engines then and there. If this was gonna be a rematch, then he wasn't going to make the same mistakes he had last time.

The gunnery booth went dead immediately, going limp in Frank's arms. "Guns are down! I repeat, total system failure! Come in, Duncan! *Piece of shit radio!"*

Another rush of static, but Duncan resisted the memories this time. He could hear Frank panting, exhausted from his white knuckle sniping. From a lifetime of death.

"Frank, come in. I've got a plan. Meet me on the flight deck. I know what to do this time. We're gonna burn 'em out."

Frank punched the computer console in frustration. "The armory's too far away, it's clear on the other end of the ship. We can't get there, there's no time!"

"That's fine, we'll work our way over to resupply." Duncan stopped pacing abruptly. "What do we have on hand?"

Frank patted down his suit. "I've got my sawed-off, two boxes of shells next to the nav computer, bandolier on the seat behind you, a few heat rays runnin' low, my utility knife — that's about it for weapons."

Duncan closed his eyes and focused hard. "Tools, I need tools. *Options.*"

"Computer, lock it down, and kill the power." Frank stood up too fast, and almost fell back down again. "Duncan, this won't work. They'll mob the ship, surround us, that acid eats away at metal, don't matter what kind!"

Duncan nodded thoughtfully, before raising one polite finger. "We're not gonna give them that kind of time. It's about controlling the flow of traffic. Hundreds, *thousands* of Problems flying towards us. Can't fight a war on all sides." He pointed the finger at Frank. "So you lock it down, *like you just did*, and make *The Apollo* absolutely impenetrable. They're runnin' laps outside looking for any nook or cranny to slug their way into. We taunt them, rile 'em up if we can — then we *make a mistake*."

He smirked, finally finding his groove again. "Give them an opening, an edge. Just crack one window, give 'em a minute to stream inside — *the escape pod,* Frank! Filled with dynamite. We slam the window shut and I cut 'em loose. You hop back on the guns and light 'em up."

Frank punched the air. It hurt less than the walls. "Well hot damn, Dunko. That's a fuckin' plan if I ever heard one! You picked a good time to wake up."

Duncan was still locked in. "Gotta troubleshoot, strafe around the problem. See every angle, every flaw." He closed his eyes, trying to visualize the whole plan. "There's gotta be *one* hole in the ship. Has to be. And they'll find it too. Eating *The Clunker*, now that's an education. It's a masterwork of engineering, teach them everything they need to know." He shook his head clear and looked up at Frank like he'd just remembered he was there.

"You're a little fucked up, ya know that?"

Duncan bowed. "The heat rays, can you shoulder mount them?"

"Uh — briefly, sure. Why not?"

"Perfect. Two of them on me, you keep the other one and your sawed-off. That's where you're strongest. I'm gonna need the knife though."

Frank's eyebrows disappeared under his bandana. "I told ya, kid, they eat straight through metal, like hot sauce through stomach lining."

"I know, but the only luck I've had against these fucks is up close. Melee range." Duncan took the knife Frank was holding out for him. "Alright, that should work. Need two patrols. I'll make my way to the armory and resupply. You take this half of the ship — gotta keep you close to the guns."

He jumped down from the table and nodded stiffly at Frank. "That work for you? Sorry if I — I know it's your ship."

"We're in this thing together, kid, I told ya. And that right there, that was Captain's work. Let's ride."

They suited up and split off, linking up radio comms and — for the very first time — shaking hands. But Frank and Duncan were not the only *beings* creeping through *The Apollo* at that very moment.

The very first Problem to touch down on the ship was Lemmy. He had soared through space with his — you know. *It was all held high*, in spirit. He was a gallant general leading his troops into battle, a proud liberator marching upon the enemy stronghold. Like Washington crossing the — that river, in the painting, hands on his hips, all sassy, fully intact head held high. It was just like that, but with one bloodshot eyeball and a million green blobs. More teeth than in the painting too, and none of them wooden.

Lemmy was painfully aware that his time was running short. Never mind his father and his brothers, if he screwed up again then there was an excellent chance that his troops would turn on him. Mutiny, every leader's worst nightmare. But he would prove them wrong, all of them. He was a master strategist, up against two nobodies. In a few minutes, with a tight enough seal, this ship would be his. Then, he would take charge of the whole wretched mass, absorb the strength and power of both ships and every soldier he had available to him. *No more humans.* And then, when his father arrived, who knows what might happen? Perhaps it was time for a changing of the guard.

He raced along the outside of the ship, feeling for any slight give in the hull. He had to kill the humans himself. After what they had done to him, of course he did. To avenge himself, to earn the respect of his subordinates. To make sure that they were truly and properly dead, once and for all.

Lemmy felt his cornea swell up and he stopped dead. Very slowly, he began to backtrack. It felt like a maintenance hatch. A handle, a thin window, a series of screws and bolts, and then he found it. There would be an airlock to deal with inside, but he would figure that out in due time. This was enough for now, not for everyone, but certainly for him — the much underestimated eyeball. He alone could fit through this keyhole, *undetected*.

Less than two feet from Lemmy, at this very moment, was Duncan. His left hand was free, and his right hand gripped Frank's worn utility knife. The heat rays on his shoulders were set to activate automatically when the sensors picked up even one strand of Problem DNA.

His voice was a hoarse whisper over the radio. "Frank, you see anything yet?"

"Negative. Computer's goin' nuts, the ship is totally overrun. We're down to our eyeballs, kid."

"What about the intercom? Is that still up?"

"Sure thing. You havin' problems with yer radio?"

Duncan jumped, but it was just another shadow. "It's not that. On *The Clunker*, I was broadcasting over the intercom. Taunting the Problem. I don't even know if it spoke English, but it seemed to piss it off pretty good."

As you will no doubt remember, Problems speak about as much English as Frank speaks Russian. Which is to say, of course —

"None, to my knowledge anyway. And I'd know. But tone, volume, spittle — you're right, they do seem to register all that shit. It's a good idea, and actually — "

Static crackled through Duncan's helmet and set his teeth on edge. "Frank! Are you still there?"

"Yeah, sorry, just thinkin'. Down on the moon, in the tunnels, the 'Problems' almost — just for a second there — they almost seemed to know what I was thinking. Or sayin', screamin', the meanin' of the whole thing. Might not be a bad idea. Maybe we'll cross some wires, send 'em a few mixed messages, just in case."

Duncan slapped his helmet. "Radio's cutting out a little here, Frank. Problems, down on the moon? More than one?"

"Oh a shitload. Some sort of colony. Thought I cleared them out, couple times, but you know how they are."

Duncan stepped on a grate to stop it rattling — only to realize that his whole body was trembling. "It makes sense. They must communicate with each other, especially if they're workin' spaceships and launching special ops. Someone's doin' all that, but I've never heard anything like a *word* come out of 'em."

"Can't be usin' radios either, they'd eat right through 'em."

"So maybe it's telepathic. Brain radios, you know? Why not? Who knows what these little pricks are capable of?" Duncan adjusted his grip on the knife. "Let's proceed under that assumption, for now anyway. A hive mind. *Makes your mixed message idea more promising.*"

"I'm on it. You let me know when you hit the armory. Stay frosty, Dunko. Radio out."

Duncan flicked a switch on the neck of his suit and cut his radio too. Didn't need Frank hearing him hyperventilate up and down the halls of *The Apollo*. He hadn't seen anything yet. Not a blur or a shadow, not a thimble full of murderous green goo. And to be honest, he was almost disappointed, until he reminded himself that his plan might actually be working. No loose Problems wandering the ship could mean that they were all being funneled into the *highly explosive* escape pod.

A flash of light caught his eye, but it was just a reflection. Still, he felt the knife shaking in his hand. A patch of bright shiny metal in the distance — what was it? He approached cautiously, and then an overhead light came on very suddenly. He just barely kept control of his bladder. This wasn't an ambush, he had just gotten turned around. This was the pantry, he'd seen it before, on the way to discovering that disastrous trophy room.

"Alright — *tools*, come on Duncan." The hot sauce, that Frank used for his special ammo. What had he called it, *habanero* something. It didn't matter. Frank thought they could feed it through the filtration system, stream it through the vents and liquify the Problems — if things got real bad.

Duncan scanned the shelves, but he didn't see anything orange. Most everything was expired, or random. Useless. Some flour though, a dozen synthetic eggs — his eyes quickly darted between the ingredients he knew, ignoring everything else. Sugar, salt, butter — by god, he even had lemons. Duncan had to grab the doorframe to steady himself. Could this be true? He had everything, *every ingredient one would require to make a —*

"Son of a bitch! Oh that's even worse than finding everything just sitting here right before we get eaten! One fucking — cornstarch?"

He spluttered incoherently for a moment, trying and failing to calm down. "Of all things, he's missing fucking *cornstarch?* Not that I have my space oven to cook it in anyway. Nope! Took that from me too, didn't they? Blew it to shit, *with me inside it!* That was a neat trick. My burned-out pride and joy, cruelly abandoned on the surface of the moon. Like common waste. And what did we find there anyway? Every rock we turn over has more fucking Problems under it!"

He was hitting his stride now, and more importantly, his hand had stopped shaking. "No more, I tell you! I've had more than enough of all this! One way or another, *this will end today* — you mark my words!"

With renewed vigor, he turned to continue his patrol route towards the armory — but epiphany hit him like a steam train. It was an unworthy 'eureka moment,' the breakthrough of a feeble but *creative* mind. He sprinted down the hall, muttering and whispering like a lunatic, really trying to cover his bases before he presented the new plan to Frank.

And just on the other side of the wall, perhaps two feet away, was a Problem moving at high speed, in the *opposite* direction. On a sudden whim, just as the tail end of his pathetic eyeball body was slipping through the keyhole, Lemmy has reached out and lassoed an unsuspecting soldier.

Through sheer force of will, he destroyed the lesser Problem. A single wave of electric hatred was all it took, a truly and literally cancerous blast of malice. The soldier short-circuited and went limp as Lemmy drank the rest of his delicious body through the keyhole. And when he hit the floor, wouldn't you know it — Lemmy was whole once again.

Frank's voice crackled out over the intercom, sounding somewhat more *polite* than usual. "New plan, my expansive crew and I — their ingenious Captain, are going to regroup in the escape pod for immediate evacuation! Operation — uh, Operation Delta Foxtrot is a go!"

Lemmy was crackling with a sick, rabid glee. The others would find an opening. The cavalry would be stampeding through these shabby halls any minute now. But first, he would *feed.* The human was here, the one with the bandana and the secrets, *he could feel it in his jellies.* Oh, and he recognized his voice on the intercom.

"Wouldn't it be a shame if someone tracked us down and devoured us all — in the starboard supply closet where we're all hiding out together, unarmed and unawares?"

Lemmy melted through the wall of the airlock and tumbled faster and faster, until he was rocketing down the hallway towards that faint *signal* he smelled in the air. He *knew* this monster now. He'd seen him with his own eye, and now he could actually smell him. Ah, to have nostrils once again — it was divine. Lemmy was reborn, reforged in the fires of his own mind. Things would be different this time, he knew it. This body would serve him well, crackling with energy and youth — not to mention all these glorious teeth.

And as our two vengeful ships pass each other in the endless night, each blissfully unaware of the other's presence or proximity, we are forced to make a narrative choice. Let's follow Duncan, his thoughts don't require as much translation, and I'm curious to hear more about this cornstarch thing.

"Frank, I've got something for ya! Come in, over."

Another snowstorm fell on Duncan's ears. Roaring static, interrupted by grunts — the sounds of a struggle. He missed a step and almost fell back into his memories.

"Frank? Fuck, I'm on my way — hold on!"

Duncan spun around and broke into a full-tilt sprint. His breath started to fog up his helmet and he blew past the supply closets and sleeping quarters. He punched a stitch in his side that popped up near the pantry, and then he exploded back onto the flight deck.

"Frank! Where are — "

The words caught in his throat. He heard a beep that he didn't recognize, and then he saw Frank, swaying unsteadily in his boots. He was injured. There was blood on the *inside* of his helmet, and one arm was bent back the wrong way — but he was still breathing.

"Nice of you to join us, *Captain*. 'Fraid you missed the fun." His legs gave out and Frank crumpled to the ground. "Fuckin' knees! Come help me up, I'll be alright."

"The Problem, Frank, where is it? Is it dead?"

Frank laughed, and then grunted against the pain. Without waiting for the requested assistance, he clamored back up to his feet and leaned heavily against the table.

"Oh you know I got him." He waved like a particularly old and tired matador, and Duncan's eyes refocused on the small rectangular machine on the shelf behind Frank. So *that's* where the beep had come from.

"Is that a *microwave?*"

"A *space* microwave, top of the line model. Well, it was. I'm sure he's ruined it by now."

Through the ugly little dot matrix layered over the viewing window, Duncan could just barely see roiling ugly shadows. Some small part of him registered how admittedly sleek and impressive the appliance looked.

Might've been part of the same line as his space oven. "Did you — you know — "

"Not yet. Too risky to turn it on. They feed off the energy, you know. *Boom.*" He looked suddenly very old indeed. "Tried that one before, didn't work out so great. Regardless, I'm thinkin' we use it like bait. Part of your cattle-herdin' strategy, pushin' em all towards the escape pod. You know, we *threaten* to kill it. Use the intercom, but the sawed-off too — through the window. Send a message in the universal language. If you're right about the hive-mind, that might get through to 'em. And worst case, they don't care and we fry him anyway."

"Contingency."

"Redundancy. *Insurance.*"

"I like it."

Frank shot him a wincing smile. "Thought you might. Speakin' of which, right before this little bastard arrived, I got confirmation. Escape pod's full up."

"Well I'm glad you brought that up, actually. I was doin' some thinking on my patrol — I had an idea." Duncan holstered Frank's knife. "We've been trying to kill these things, which is a damn sight harder than I thought it would be. Passed the pantry, checked for your hot sauce — no luck. But it got me thinking. What if, instead of just killing them, maybe *in addition* to trying to kill them, what if we tried to weaken them?"

Frank was unconvinced. "Seems like a lot of work. Killin' works pretty good."

"But if we weaken them first, disarm them, *de-fang them*, they might be easier to kill." Duncan was talking with his hands, really trying to sell his idea. "Say we load up the exhaust, the vents — hell, the guns too — with an accelerant of sorts, that — when it comes into contact with heat — doesn't just burn 'em, but *bakes* 'em. Wouldn't it be easier to hunt pastries than Problems?"

"You're losing me here, kid. You hungry?"

"No, Frank, I'm an amateur baker, in my — free time." He shook the distraction loose and pressed on. "We salvage a good amount of *cornstarch*, hit up a transport ship, drop down to Earth and build up a real stockpile, then we take their knees out from under them, forever. *We end this.*"

"I appreciate the thought, but that's impossible."

"It's not! Cornstarch is — I think it's some sort of leavening agent, or it activates a glucose, yeast thing that would neutralize the electricity inside the Problems."

"It's not possible, Duncan! Forget about it. You can't de-fang these creatures." Frank stood up gingerly. "They come back, they *always* come back. And Earth — there's nothin' left, nothin' they didn't take."

"What do you mean? It's probably all just been sitting there since evac. Mint condition, we can hit up as many supermarkets as we want, *load up!*"

Frank shook his head sadly. "Duncan, they didn't evacuate Earth because of a tear in the atmosphere."

"Yes, they did — *I was there, Frank!*"

"I'm sorry, kid."

Frank almost collapsed again in a fit of thick, blood-spattered coughing. Duncan ran forward to help him, and steadied them both by placing a hurried hand on the counter. Unfortunately, his hand landed on the *mute button* for the ship computer.

"IN REVERSE CHRONOLOGICAL ORDER, SATURN, MARS, DELTA CENTAURI, MERCURY, VENUS, PLUTO, GANYMEDE — "

"Duncan, shut that shit off, please!"

The computer blared louder, as if it resented the Captain's interruption. "NEPTUNE, MOON, AND ORIGINATING ON THE PLANET EARTH."

Frank leaned over and punched the mute button himself.

Duncan's voice was quiet. "What was that?"

Frank slapped the back of the monitor. "Heat tracking signature, for the Problems."

Duncan frowned, confused and nervous in a way that he couldn't explain. He reach out to Frank, who was more or less draped across the desk at this point.

Bzzzt! Buzzzt!

The heat rays on his shoulders whirred to life and blasted the navigation computer apart. Duncan threw himself to the side to avoid hitting Frank.

"Dammit, what was — Frank, how do I turn these things off?"

"I'm sorry, kid."

Numbly, Duncan turned back towards Frank, and felt the heat rays start to spin up again. He was whispering to himself, putting the last pieces of the puzzle into place. "Organic lifeforms, composition unknown. You've been hunting Problems since — before evac. Decades. And they haven't killed you, all this time."

"Duncan, please — let me." He strained against his broken body and stood up straight. There wasn't just blood and bile in his throat, but guilt too. He had to let it out, he had to tell Duncan everything.

Frank opened his mouth, and his mind faded back to that pivotal first rematch, after *Apollo 11* exiled them in space. The catastrophic journey through the atmosphere had split them apart, but from that very first moment they escaped gravity, it had hunted him.

The tumor wanted to find him. Every day and every night. It didn't sleep, it didn't even rest. It hunted him — whether for revenge or simple hunger, he never knew. But it always came back, no matter where he ran to. No matter where he flew in the galaxy, it followed him.

So eventually, when he had made his peace with death, Frank let it catch up to him. He strapped himself into a patchy, handmade space suit and flew right out to meet it. That familiar snarl, the flash of those teeth. He met death head on and surrendered to it. The tumor had flown at his head, screeching so sharply that a crack appeared in his helmet. And Frank had closed his eyes.

But the creature didn't eat his brain. No, the tumor burned through the spacesuit and snuggled back into the dent in his head. He felt another part of it worming back into his chest cavity, exactly where — of course — it used to live. It purred and settled, matching his breathing. And Frank felt his heart rate begin to slow. He felt himself begin to fade. He felt that old anger coming back, burning through every good thought he'd ever had.

And that's when he flicked the lighter on, but it didn't catch. His homemade space suit, a fireproof iron maiden that was supposed to burn up both him *and* his tumor once and for all — failed. The tumor gurgled and roared, ripping at his chest. Tearing at his organs, flaying his skin.

Frank kicked and spun, screaming out into the void. His eyeballs nearly burst from the pain, and only muscle memory got him to the sawed-off. He fired and fired until his whole field of vision was a constellation of floating shells and exploding stars. But the tumor did not die. He didn't know for years what had been real and what had been hallucination, an agonized vision clouding his memory, but there was no mistaking it now.

The tumor had split, like so much mercury, into clusters of death. Dozens of enraged, burning fragments, twisted fractures of himself. And he had passed out, watching them spread out all around him. His vision had blurred, his body had started to patch itself back together, and in his last conscious moments, Frank had watched his tumors spiral off and spread throughout the galaxy.

In subsequent years he had pieced together three initial waves. One floated into open space and whack-a-mole infected a thousand hidden pockets of the universe. Another spun towards the moon, which he had purged a hundred times over, to no avail. And the last wave had landed on Earth, to apocalyptic consequence.

Frank felt his pulse heavy and throbbing in his skull, like an alarm clock. A reminder of what he had done, how he had doomed the whole galaxy, for all eternity. And he finally returned to *The Apollo,* and saw Duncan's betrayed face staring back at him.

"You — but. No. The Problems, the — your question when we met. Contact with — *it always comes back.* But evac — an accident at work." His voice fell flat, and eyes grew wide. "Military hospital. A test pilot. It was a freak — freak accident."

"Duncan, you *should* be mad. You have every right." Frank broke into a wheeze and punched his chest until it stopped. "Let it all out, I can take it."

Duncan moved back, seemingly without meaning to, as his mouth formed the words.

"You killed my father."

Chapter Nine: <u>The Apollo</u>

For his part, Lemmy was getting pretty hot under the collar. He didn't know exactly what a microwave *was*, but that whiff of artificial electricity was setting off some vague alarm bells just the same. And no one likes to be stuck in a cage. But even worse was this *spectacle* the humans were staging outside. The yelling and crying, the dramatic pauses, sharp inhales of breath, it was all very operatic — and quite besides the point.

They had bested him, *once again,* but for some reason they were now just completely ignoring him. The human had sensed his approach, somehow, and spun around with all sorts of dreadful weaponry aimed at his beautiful new body. Lemmy had acted without hesitation, with an agility and speed that he never could've managed before. And still, it didn't matter. The signal-emitting, secret-keeping old human had been faster. Shooting, kicking, grumbling all the while — things only settled down when the door to his strange prison had slammed shut in his face.

It was altogether too much, the last straw of his grand humiliation. And so Lemmy did the only thing he could — he fired out a volley of his own signals ordering his soldiers to complete the boarding process and converge on his location. But, at this point, who knew if they could even hear him anymore.

"He's not going anywhere, that door is three or four different alloys. Duncan — "

"What? *What now?*"

Frank flinched and squeezed his eyes shut. "Nothing. I'm sorry, I told you. I've been trying to make this right for forty years now. I didn't — *it's not me*. It's the tumor."

"Tumor, Problem, Creature — I don't care what you call it. It's your DNA. It's part of *you*. You're a murderer." Duncan's eyes flashed. "More than that, millions of deaths — whole *planets*, Frank!"

"I understand why you would think that — and I'm sorry about your father, I'll say it again. I'll say it a hundred more times. He was a good man, and a good doctor too, *but — "*

"I'm not interested in your apologies! I don't even know who the fuck I'm even talking to right now! You killed my crew! You blew up my ship!" Duncan took an unconscious step back. "And how do I even know there's a 'Frank' left in there? *You're just a Problem in skin suit!"*

"Duncan — I did not do those things. The tumor did."

"It's *your* DNA! Ask the computer!"

Frank took off his helmet. "First of all — it's barely a calculator, that I built and wired with my own two hands, decades ago. But yes, the creatures do share my DNA. But I am not my — tumors. I am sick. I *was* sick, I am — I don't know exactly what I am now." He spat more blood onto the counter. "But I am still human, just like you."

"How do I know that? Why should I believe you, about anything? You ruined my life, bit by bit, crushed it up into a fine powder and blew it into the wind!"

Frank pointed at the microwave and spoke through gritted teeth. "That *thing* is not me! *I* rescued you from space, I have saved you — *we* have saved each other, a dozen times over! Has that *fucking TUMOR* ever done anything but hurt you?"

Another revelation quietly fell into place for Duncan, like birdshit splattering on a brand new hat. "You said it spread through all these pockets of the galaxy, said it was this horrible threat, but you kept a few in your office?"

"Research, Duncan. The more I know about them, the more of them I can kill, and the faster I can do it."

"*And what a bang up job you've done so far!*"

Frank felt the old anger burning inside him again. "You tell me, why isn't this whole universe one big green pile of shit?"

"I don't know, the tumors are sickly, or slow. They're running a slow sweep of the whole galaxy while you — watch for threats." Duncan held Frank's gaze. "Distract onlookers and dispatch woebegone Captains — "

"No, you stupid prick. The only reason that your 'Problems' haven't eaten every planet you can name is because I spend every waking moment hunting them. *Me!* I rejected them, they don't want me anymore. In the jars, my office, they hide from me when I approach." His voice was a rasping plea. "*They claw at the glass to get away from me. No — their mission's different now. New hosts, new victims. They* don't want me, Duncan — they want everything else."

Frank closed his eyes and slammed his arm against the wall, turning his elbow back the right way round and popping his shoulder back into place. "I trained the computer to track them, to track our *shared* DNA. But those fucking things are not me. I was a test pilot! I wanted to serve my country, to go to space. *To explore — "*

Frank waved his arms around, wincing at the pain. "And just look at me now, livin' the dream." He stared darkly at Duncan, his lips still tight. "Computer, release escape pod, full force on rear thrusters. Put some distance between us and them, *please*."

Duncan felt the ship jerk forwards as the escape pod blasted off. More and more mental birdshit was piling up. He didn't know what to say. He didn't know what to think. If he had a breaking point, they had to be approaching it now — right? *The Clunker* swam at the edges of his vision, and Frank's voice sounded like it was coming from the end of a long hallway.

"Computer, scan the ship for remaining tumors. Duncan, my arm is shot. You take the guns, finish out your plan. It's a stack of dynamite up to the ceiling, shouldn't take more than a few shots."

He gestured towards the gunnery booth, but Duncan didn't move. His eyes were blank with shock. "The heat rays. You knew. Mounting them to my shoulders, attaching the sensors, you knew this would happen."

"Yeah, so what? I wasn't going to send you out there without protection. Please, the guns. They won't be in range long." Frank hesitated, for just a moment. "Then we can talk."

Duncan jogged over to the cannons and strapped himself in. He made contact on the third shot, and the explosion was so blindingly bright that he had to turn away from it. A fireball of scorched metal — and right on the edges, tendrils of jagged, nasty lightning. But no shade of green anywhere — not a single blip or blob.

Duncan caught himself whispering again, to no one in particular. "*It worked.*" He didn't feel anything at the realization. No satisfaction, no relief, no sudden rush of — anything. Duncan felt numb.

His hand went to his neckline and flipped on the radio. "Problem solved. The escape pod is gone. No sign of any survivors."

"That's great to hear, kid. It was all you."

Duncan closed his eyes and let himself be carried off by the static. "You don't look sick, Frank." There was a long delay, but Duncan didn't move. He didn't want to have this conversation face to face.

"I know. Some days I feel pretty good. And they never gave me any treatment. Just got rid of the evidence, fired me into space and kept on whistlin'. It ain't any normal type of cancer, I've read everythin' I could. This is somethin' else. I don't know what it is, I don't know how to fix it, but I know I'm dyin'. I can feel that much. Maybe that's some small comfort to you. To everyone who's lost so much. But I told you before, *and I meant it too, Dunko.*"

Frank tried for a deep exhale, but the breath caught in his throat. "I'm takin' these fuckers with me. Many as I can, I promise you that."

The radio flipped off again, and Duncan stared out into the void. His eyes widened, pupils dilating against the growing darkness. The shrapnel of the escape pod was scattering out of sight. He could see the abandoned *Clunker* breaking apart too. And tears burned in his eyes, but not for a spaceship.

"PLANETARY MOVEMENT DETECTED."

Duncan heard the computer through Frank's radio, but it didn't make sense. He squinted around, swinging the cannon sights, scanning with the instruments — but there was nothing there. Space, stars, debris. That was it!

"What's the computer talking about, Frank?"

"Checkin' it out — as we speak. Hold on, it's got somethin' over — no, *come on now*. Do you feel that?"

"Feel what? You're freakin' me out here, Frank."

"Like the gravity in — in the ship. It's too high, ratcheting — computer, stabilize internal grav field."

"ALL INTERIOR BAROMETRICS CURRENTLY STABLE."

"Bullshit! Told you this thing was a fuckin' calculator. Reset all internal barometrics, *immediately!* Dunko, you gotta get over here."

"ALL INTERIOR BAROMETRICS CURRENTLY STABLE, EXCEPT FOR THE CAPTAIN'S HEARTBEAT."

Duncan had to strain his ears to make out Frank's words. "I would have seen this — it's not a 'bad' computer, just got some quirks. Blind spots, but not this fuckin' big! It's Jupiter!"

When Duncan finally made his way back to the flight deck, he saw Frank bent over, clutching his chest. Nothing was wrong with the air pressure or gravity or whatever.

"Frank — what's goin' on?"

"I would have seen it! I trace their heat signatures, you've heard me do it. They *nest*, Duncan, they colonize and cluster and dig their way through whole moons in a single afternoon. There are always traces, *always*, straight lines all the way back to the first one. Back to me!"

Duncan had never seen Frank so *out* of control. It was like looking in a mirror. "Slow down — what 'planetary movement' is happening? Is it more Problems? Is this about Earth?"

"No, it's — *gah!*" He reared back like a wild horse. Duncan had no idea how to help. Frank was squeezing his head, his fingers were turning white.

"PLANETARY   MOVEMENT   DETECTED, APPROACHING THE APOLLO."

Frank forced his eyes open. His hands were moving in slow motion, it was like some of the signals from his brain were getting lost in transit. He growled through his teeth and fought to pull up his shirt. "It's all of them. Don't know how but — all of them, they're all coming."

"CONTACT IMMINENT."

"Contact with what? *With what? With whom? Explain!*" Duncan continued to scream at the charmingly retro computer — lots of green lights, that old typewriter font, all manner of knobs and twiddles and dials — but if we pan around the scene, past Duncan and Frank and the computer, we'll find someone tucked away in a top of the line space microwave who — for an absolute certainty — knows the answers to all of these burning questions.

Lemmy felt that pull deep down in his core around the same time Frank did, but, of course, nobody was checking in with him. No one cared what Lemmy thought. It wasn't just the total defeat and humiliation of his pointless existence that irked him in this moment — it was the disrespect.

No, he didn't speak the language, but they could make an effort. Or they could just kill him, in many ways that would be better.

To die in battle against a sworn enemy, now that was something to be proud of! But to be so unceremoniously *benched*, nothing but a forgotten passenger on the great journey? No. He would not be luggage.

The older human tore at his spacesuit, and only Lemmy was unsurprised by what was revealed beneath it. Stabbing, boiling fingers of green acid thrust out from his chest, scrabbling for a grip on his arms. The younger human lashed out at them, hooting and hollering like an idiot. Big mistake.

Lemmy drooled against the microwave door as the remaining, newly reawakened scraps of Problem within Frank's chest turned away from the attacking Duncan, reaching inward for easier targets. From his many years of feeding on humans, Lemmy knew exactly what sort of snacks his brothers would find. Delicious organs, sweet rivers of blood — he had to stop before he got lightheaded.

"You — Problem, in the microwave — what're you, a scout? A diversion? *Where are the rest of you?* You've got five seconds!" Duncan raised one dramatic finger to hover next to the 'start' button. "Let's see if you glow in the dark! Tell me what's goin' on!"

Lemmy didn't respond *verbally,* but he glared hot death at Duncan.

"Wait — I *know* you, you little shit!"

"CONTACT IMMINENT."

"Shut up! Not now." Duncan punched the computer. It hurt, but hey — if Frank could put holes in the wall, he could step into the ring with a scrapyard monitor. "You — that eye, your left eye. Frank, this is the one that took out *The Clunker*. The one I lost on — *on the space oven*."

Frank was nearly unconscious, his every muscle and blood cell working overtime to survive the sudden, barbaric end of his remission.

"That's it. Frank — the computer didn't pick up on whatever this Jupiter thing is because it's *mutated*. Evolved. You said you rejected it and so it then rejected you." He bent down and lifted Frank up onto the table. "You are *not* your cancer, Frank. I was wrong. It's not even your DNA anymore."

Frank struggled to speak through the pain. "This one *is* though — I can feel it. It's the first one, the one that fled. From my chest, the first tumor."

"Hell of a time for your homecoming." Duncan glared back at Lemmy. "Lime tart *my ass!*"

Frank coughed, and it sounded like a car backfiring. "What's that, Dunko?"

Before Duncan could reply, a Goliath roar shuddered through *The Clunker*. It was a horrendous, boundless sound that shook our Captains' eyeballs and rang garglingly in their ears.

"PLANETARY ARRIVAL."

Duncan whirled around, expecting to see a stream of Problems barreling down the hallway. But the ship was clear. The hallway was empty. What *wasn't* empty was the big porthole window, through which, he finally saw the thing that used to be Jupiter. The *Big Problem,* that first and utmost dilemma which has plagued our heroes through both time and space. It was a writhing, vile mass of tumors so large that it could swallow up *The Apollo* in one bite and not even have to burp afterwards.

A delighted snurgle escaped Lemmy. You know what they say, one man's death trap is another alien cancer monster's estranged floating home hive mind. Lemmy would never admit this, but for a flashing moment he felt *grateful* for his microwave prison. The tint of the glass meant that his father *probably* hadn't seen that shudder of horror that passed through him. There was nowhere left to turn now. Nowhere to run, nowhere to hide. This was it.

"Oh shit. Shit shit shit — Frank, do we fight it or do we run?" Duncan glanced down at Frank, but the old man was fighting his own battle right now. There was foam at the corners of his mouth. "*Got it.* I'll — if you don't mind. I got this." And then he found himself whispering again. "Come on, Captain."

"ORGANIC LIFE FORMS DETECTED. HOSTILE. COMPOSITION UNKNOWN."

"*No shit!* Computer — evasive maneuvers, defense shield — do *something* useful, and do it quietly!" Duncan ran over to the gunnery booth. "Wrong side of the ship. No line of sight. Alright."

The Apollo lurched to one side and he heard the buzzing of what he *hoped* was some sort of advanced shielding system. Duncan ran over to the cockpit and tried to repress the terrified smile that was starting to form in the corner of his mouth.

"Not now, *I'm busy.* We're gonna take damage on the way out, there's too much debris out there. But if that thing catches us, the — I dunno, *Big* Problem — if it catches us, we're dead and buried."

Duncan punched the flight controls and strapped himself in. "Half a tank of fuel. We can outrun it, for a while anyway. But if it's got Frank's scent — *it always comes back.*"

He grabbed the steering wheel, only momentarily stopping to appreciate the retro-futuristic flourishes. It felt like one of those old muscle cars from the movies. Leather accents, crisp lining, molded handles. This really was quite a ship.

A weak voice came in over the radio. "Duncan — "

"Don't worry about a thing. I got this. Lay back down, or find a seat somewhere. We could be doin' barrel rolls in a minute here." Duncan's mind raced ahead of *The Apollo*. He knew his objective, his limited toolset, he knew his enemy. *What was he missing?*

"Frank, if you can hear me, if you can respond — is this thing hunting for sport? Are we just the next meal?"

The Big Problem roared again, and Duncan almost lost control of the ship. He could feel his brain sloshing around in his head. It was sickening.

"Could be that, or revenge. I'm still alive, for now, and that's no good for them. And like I told you before, we got a captive. In the microwave, maybe they want him back."

Duncan flipped a half dozen switches, settling in. "Will it chase him instead of us? Say we toss him out a side window and bolt, what do you think?"

"No, it's a good idea but we're a better target." Frank growled, fighting a sudden head rush. "I can get to the guns, just spin her around."

"No, Frank! Save your strength, I need your *knowledge* now. Nobody knows these things better than you."

"That's nice, kid, but I'm not challengin' this thing to a foot race. They're pure momentum, no way we win that one."

Lemmy was doing his very best to melt through the door of the space microwave, and making no progress at all. It was the same story with the side walls, but then he spotted a grill towards the back. Must be where the power came through. He slammed his whole body weight into the back of the appliance and *pushed*, burning bright against his cage, oozing through every crevice.

Duncan was wagging a finger victoriously, struck by his own genius. "We don't need it to chase us *forever*, just long enough to string 'em along into a trap."

Frank was intrigued. "What's your plan?"

Duncan saw a tooth flash by on the rear-view mirror. His perspective was all off, it was his first time piloting this strange and particular ship, but the tooth seemed to be roughly the same size as the space station he grew up on.

"Same as ever, Frank. *Burn 'em out.* Computer — redirect all power to the engines, full throttle. Set course for the sun. Pure momentum, eh? Well, I've got a hell of a dodge."

Frank's voice was strained, but not unkind. "It's too far."

"ERROR. INSUFFICIENT FUEL."

"I heard him, *thank you!*" Duncan hoped Frank was hitting the computer on his behalf. His thoughts were interrupted by a fresh wave of titanic, labored panting from the Big Problem. "What can we cut loose? No time to stop for gas here, Frank!"

"It's not that simple — or maybe it is. Good thinkin'. Here, I need the main computer focused on incoming damage, projectiles — you know — "

The Apollo flew into a corkscrew spiral, and Duncan saw a thick knotted limb of Problem gloop soar past them. "Oh great, a planet with arms. Like a fat little T-rex."

Duncan caught himself murmuring again, but he couldn't hear Frank clearly anymore. All that electricity from the Big Problem must have been interfering with the signal.

Frank's voice mingled with the static, blurring and grating against Duncan's eardrums. "But there's a secondary nav system in the — office next to the gunnery. You head over there and chart a course. I'll make preparations."

Duncan punched the steering wheel. "No way, I'm faster than the autopilot. It's about reaction speed, Frank, twitch reflexes — "

"Don't argue, please!" Frank was wheezing bad. "Just trust me."

Duncan cursed and climbed out of the cockpit. This felt too familiar, but he didn't feel any more prepared than last time. An empty spaceship, one rabid alien, death all around him. What had he called it, on *The Clunker?* Operation Pelican, his big brainwave, rambled out over the intercom to a couple dozen of his closest corpses. And how was this any different? A space race into the sun, they'd burn up on the approach, *if* the ship even made it that far. *Operation Phoenix*, another thundering dud.

The Apollo spun into another whirling dive, but this time the ship did a full one-eighty and completely reversed course. They were flying towards the Big Problem!

"Computer, what the — "

He turned back to re-enter the flight deck, but then Duncan saw Frank through the window in the door. He was strapped into the cockpit.

"I'm sorry, kid. Like you said — contingency." And he hit the button, the *break-glass-in-case-of-emergency* button that Duncan didn't even know about. The back door of *The Apollo* sprang open and just about everything flew out. It was a maelstrom of salvaged food from the pantries, pilfered weaponry from the armory, and Captain Duncan Arugula — all sucked out into open space and cast off into infinity. It was like one big toilet flush.

Frank had made his final preparations while Duncan was flying the ship. There was no need to preserve his energy anymore, nothing to hold back for. First, he had slipped out of the flight deck and into the pantry. Duncan was onto something with that cornstarch idea, but it was too explosive an idea for them to try together. No, this was *his* mess to clean up.

Next, he had grabbed a few more supplies and relics and hurried back to the flight deck. Duncan was still talking to himself, and didn't suspect a thing. Lemmy saw everything, of course, but no one cared about Lemmy.

"You don't have to do this! Frank, you've already sacrificed yourself." Duncan screamed his throat ragged over the radio. "You are not your tumors! This isn't your fault! Frank, let me help you!"

But Frank's radio wasn't even turned on anymore.

Chapter Ten: <u>Echo Chamber</u>

"Computer, seal up the ship. Divert all remaining power, including *all* remaining fuel, to ventilation. Reverse polarity on the air conditioning systems and overcharge the fans. Kill the engines — and turn this thing into a vacuum." Frank walked over to the space microwave, feeling an unexpected levity wash over him. The hard part was over.

"And how have *you* been doin', little fella? Just hangin' out in there, takin' a nap? Don't worry, you'll be back with the rest of yer kind soon enough — even me. It's gonna be a big family reunion, just you wait." He tapped on the glass, laughing in Lemmy's stupid face when he snarled back at him. Then he held up an ear of corn — and in the other hand, a bag of starch.

"Oh, it'll do in a pinch. Cornstarch is a hell of an accelerant, just like yer ole pal Dunko said. Gotta make sure we don't miss anyone. It's a big party, everyone's invited. But where we're goin' — well, he ain't makin' the journey with us. Not this time."

The fans spun up all around him. He could hear motors overclocking, he could smell that musty smell that meant the utilities were working too hard. The whole ship was vibrating, clattering against the scream of the engine. His *Apollo*, his beloved *Apollo*. Frank's ears popped — and then the vents and windows swung open, and the Big Problem started pouring into his ship like piss in a swimming pool. Frank took his seat, his Captain's chair, and flicked his radio back on.

"*There's still time!* Come in, Frank! Answer me!"

"*I'm here.*" Frank doubled over wheezing. "They're all here this time. All of 'em, in one place. It'll never happen again. A ship don't need two captains, you know that — but the universe needs more men like you. Duncan — it was an honor servin' alongside ya. Over and out."

"THE APOLLO IS SEALED. OPERATION SUCCESSFUL."

Frank opened the space microwave just enough to throw the corn and the starch inside. Lemmy tried to fight back, and jam himself in the doorway, but Frank slammed the door closed again without a second thought and cleanly sliced him in two. Duncan shouted over the radio, and Frank saluted him with one hand. With the other, he hit the start button on the microwave.

"Down with the ship."

The Apollo was annihilated in a spectacular, fiery crescendo — but to do the thing properly, we should take the explosion *beat by beat.* The first thing that happened, as I've already mentioned, was Lemmy being sliced in twain by the door of the space microwave. For the sake of clarity, we'll refer to these two new Lemmies as the *interior* Lemmy and the *exterior* Lemmy, considering their position in relation to the, once again, *top of the line* space microwave.

Lemmy — and I am here referring to the unified, full-bodied, pre-division tumor — was henceforth divided straight down the middle by the razor-sharp edge of the offending door. Luckily, since he was and remains, for this paragraph anyway, a pile of grotesque goo, his brain was somewhat free-floating. In the split, it went entirely to the *interior* Lemmy, leaving the *exterior* portion to twitch and wriggle on the counter for a few precious moments before being absorbed wholesale by the approaching goo wave which we've been calling the "Big" Problem. He was gone in an instant, gobbled and glooped back into the hive mind just as soon as he found himself urgently in the market for one. But let us now turn our attention to the still-sentient *interior* Lemmy, in the seconds which followed Frank's final insult.

When the door flew open, Lemmy had been caught most unawares. He had been doing his level best to tunnel out through the back of the accursed appliance, but then came a blinding light, as if from on high, and strange missiles began to fall. A bag of dust and then some oddly shaped grenade dinged him in the head, but they did not immediately make contact with each other — and that's what saved him.

Had the corn and starch even *grazed* one another, the very sun would have dimmed in awe as their thermonuclear armageddon rained purest habanero hellfire down upon the entire known galaxy and every far-reaching corner of unknown space. Or at least, that's what my back of the napkin calculations lead me to believe. But, as I say, stupid Lemmy intercepted the projectiles — and in so doing, *caught* the nuclear football. And this is where things got tricky.

Frank slammed the door shut again and pointedly poked the big red 'start' button — but still, the corn and the starch remained separated. The order ran through the microwave and short circuited near the back end, where Lemmy had been concentrating his tunneling efforts. Blinding halogens flared to life and the curiously anthropomorphic, perpetually aggrieved tumor began to rotate slowly on a thick glass dish.

But then a few stolen squiggles of electricity slipped through the hole he'd been burrowing, and Lemmy saw the world beyond his damnable prison disappear in a sudden inferno. *The Apollo* was gone in an instant, and with it much of the Big Problem — but not Lemmy.

He could feel himself moving, rocketing up and away from the point of ignition, but that wasn't to say that Lemmy quite *knew* what the fuck was happening to him. He knew his enemies — everyone — and he knew his mood — hungry. Beyond that, everything was just pain. The right half of his body was gone. *Half* of his brand new teeth, his right eye, his sense of balance — *gone* in an instant, and no longer transmitting any sort of signal back to his brain.

A dull, growling, spitting roar was filling the void, echoing through his mind and tingling down through his all his remaining senses. Daddy was home. And to make things worse, he had these two — *ah*. And that's when Lemmy's final, frantic plan fell into place. He rode the wave of the initial explosion up to the main stage of his beleaguered big day *spectacle* — and marshaled every last scrap of self-respect and confidence to kick open the microwave door.

The appliance crumpled apart with a singed whimper — and there was Lemmy. His blazing left eye met his father's. The Big Problem was in its final death throes. Goo was crackling. Sparks were sparking. Colossal, shattered teeth were floating off into the ether. And the Big Problem's imperious, planet-devouring stare was reduced to two runny eggs gurgling apart into vapor.

Lemmy squinted through the pain, searching for signs of life — and he found them. Two minuscule pupils, two scrabbling maggots of consciousness. And he knew they saw him too.

A despicable half smile ripped through Lemmy's dying body as he approached. His own eye grew wide in anticipation, and the hunger threatened to consume him. There he was, an acrid shadow of the father who had exiled and spurned him for so long. The hive was burning. His brothers were molten nothing, skid marks on an asteroid belt. But here *he* was too. At long last, Lemmy had come home.

He took his time, grinding and gnashing down both eyeballs in turn, feasting on every twitch of pain and life that flooded him. He grew fat with green death, choking down as much as he could. But the spark of life was fading — from all of them. He could feel it, but he could not yet *allow* it. Not this easily. Lemmy gurgled one last revolting, throaty laugh and took a deep breath. His eye closed. His stomach contracted. And the corn met the starch.

BOOM!

The Apollo was annihilated for a second time, or perhaps we'll call this one an impromptu cremation. The debris, the evidence, the keepsakes and party favors of our time aboard the ship were all evaporated in the blast, which flashed through the cosmos at approximately one quintillionth the size and scale of the Big Bang. Not quite what I was expecting, but still, it was pretty big. That's never a favorable comparison. The *point* is that each and every so called "problem" was destroyed utterly and forever. Lemmy actually *winked* out of existence, and boy did he take the rest of them with him. A self-defeating kill shot — the whole thing was painfully on-brand.

Only a few scraps *briefly* lingered behind. You know how these things go, always a few unforeseen consequences. One such fragment was discovered just a few minutes after the blast, just as the dust and starch began to clear, by a freshly bereft Duncan Arugula.

"This fucking 'space microwave' — *this* is what survives? What we *leave behind?*" Duncan knew the air was going to run out. He was going to die in a borrowed spacesuit, a million miles from anything worthwhile. "Can't even see Earth properly, for a final farewell. Nope, gotta make do with the moon — that piece of *shit* moon."

He held up a shard of glass from the microwave door. It had a bit of Problem slime on the tip — but there was nothing to worry about anymore. He watched it melt away, fading from a slime to a smear to — a memory. The blast had changed its color again, not orange or green this time, but yellow. A bright, burning yellow that — in another context — might have been beautiful, like a fresh blooming sunflower.

There was a plug too, possibly the power cord that had once been connected to that same, inescapable microwave. Duncan swung it around for a minute or two — still working through some stuff — and then mimed the act of plugging it in.

BEEP.

"No way. That was in my mind — or I'm really losin' it." The microwave readout floated by, and again, Duncan found himself unable to look away. He shouldn't care anymore, but he did. Perhaps he was just eager to be distracted. It was getting harder to breathe.

BEEP.

"Alright, that one was *definitely* in my head. There's no way! Just. No. Way." He folded his arms and turned away, but the disembodied microwave readout just kept on spinning. Lights were flashing on the panel, but if he read them — did that mean they were real? Unless this was fate, or some higher power — *reaching out to him in his time of greatest need?*

"'Fuck you'? There it goes again. *Fuck you.* Fuck me? Fuck you, pal!" He grabbed the flickering panel and brought it closer to his helmet. "Alright. If I can see a *glare,* then this might not be oxygen deprivation. Not sure if that's — better or worse, but — "

Right there in the circuits, he saw another fleck of Problem goo. Or it might have been his own brain melting out his ears. "Interesting. I wonder if — hmm." He jiggled the circuits a little. The readout buzzed and reset. "'Good morning!' Now that's more like it." He jangled the readout again. "'Fuck you' — okay. Nice way to say goodbye."

Duncan shook his head in distaste and watched the yellow speck disappear, affording not a single scrap of admiration for the circuitry's impressive translation work. "Guess that means they're really gone, huh? Hell of an exit, Frank, I gotta give you that."

He smiled sadly. "You would've hated this, my — goin' out like this." Duncan's smile widened. "You hated the moon." He looked around again, trying desperately to find a *creative solution* to this latest problem. "No space oven means no sailboat. No more surfing. *Apollo*'s gone. *Clunker* too, *let's hope*. I could try swimming, I suppose. More difficult when there's nothing to push off from. Eh. Maybe this is enough. We took 'em out. Saved the day. That's what matters — right?"

The question echoed out over the radio, and Duncan faltered. He suddenly felt very small, out here in all this — space. He looked past the moon, for the first time since their unfortunate visit, and settled on the stars. Mystery, possibility — they were all out there. The galaxy was full of adventure. *Wonder.* Not a bad way to go out, overlookin' all that.

And then he heard a cough, from nowhere and no one.

"Oh what now?" Duncan punched his helmet. "Can I not just die in peace? A nice fade to black before all the choking starts? Dead tumors tellin' me to go fuck myself, dead friends spittin' and spewin' in my ear — is some quiet melancholy too much to ask for?"

Another cough, and then a phlegmy throat clearing.

"Fine, I give up!" Duncan spun around to confront the new disturbance, but of course, once you *start* spinning in zero gravity, it becomes rather difficult to *stop.* "Oh god — *no, I will not die like* — Come on!" Something was there, he saw flashes of it every time he pirouetted back to face the son of a bitch piece of shit moon. "*Help! Help, please!*"

Duncan swung his arms around wildly. If it was a ship, he had to make himself unmissable! "I don't wanna die! Honor be damned, I'm not done! No more heroic sacrifices for Captain Arugula! *I want to live!*" And so he kept on flailing, absolutely burning through the rest of his oxygen, cuttin' snow angels in the stars. Of course, this also had the unexpected, dumb luck side effect of slowing his spinny nonsense.

"Oh — well that's a bummer." It was not a spaceship that was floating towards him. It was a space*suit*. Or, what increasingly looked like a coffin. "Poor Frank. If only you'd had time to — "

Duncan gasped. "It wasn't a cough!" The noise was coming from *inside* the suit. "Laughing? But — you're dead!" He spun the charred spacesuit around so it faced him properly, and wiped the soot off the helmet.

Frank's voice was muffled over the radio. "You gave me the idea, actually. Dredgin' up all that sad shit, gettin' me back into all those old stories."

"The iron maiden suit! Homemade, and — *fireproof!*"

"The very same." Frank smirked, and coughed again. He sounded unsteady, almost out of focus. "Nice, uh, reading comprehension there, Dunko. Sharp as the horn of a purebred — I dunno."

"Texas Longhorn?"

"Now you're gettin' a hang of it. Told ya you've been out here too long. But yes — you were right, about my grand gesture. Don't need to die to — prove ma point. And besides — I'm actually feelin' pretty good."

Duncan laughed wildly, spraying spittle on the inside of his helmet. "You sound like shit! And look worse! *Uh* — sorry. That's good to hear."

"My thoughts exactly. Sixties ain't dead, and — "

"Frank?"

"Shut up, Dunko, I'm gettin' at somethin' here." Frank grumbled deeply. "Shit's hard to — articulate, sometimes."

"I am ninety percent sure this is oxygen deprivation. Or maybe you're Mister Swan! Show me your hands."

Frank turned away, pouting. "Fine, then — never mind."

Duncan gathered himself and took a deep breath. It took two attempts. The silence stretched out between them, and Frank sounded almost nervous when he responded.

"I wanted to try livin' without cancer for a while." There was a sniffle from inside the iron maiden, but Frank covered it with a cough, that quickly turned into a wheeze.

"Still — we gotta get you to a hospital, *immediately*."

"Not a bad idea." Frank snorted. "You got a ship?"

Duncan laughed, and it was only somewhat bitter.

"Flare, on my hip." Frank sounded like he was fading again. "I can't reach it — arm got all busted up in the blast." He slurred for a moment, fighting to stay lucid. "Still, that don't make me a fuckin' swan."

Duncan's eyes settled on a shattered piece of *The Apollo*. "Yeah, good job on that, by the way. The boom."

And now it was Frank's turn to laugh. A passing supply ship saw the flare soon enough — Frank had already pinged them with his radio — and with a few whole minutes of oxygen to spare, Duncan Arugula and Frank Mustard were pulled onboard and rescued. The crew didn't believe any of their stories, but they did have a first aid kit — and that was the more timely issue.

Duncan was goin' nuts with the hand gestures again, trying to bring everyone up to speed. "No, seriously, our ships blew up, both of 'em. And mine came back for a minute, but then I guess they — let it fall apart again?

Definitely gone though. Both *obliterated*. Even the appliances, if you can believe that!"

They didn't.

"Hey — uh — you got a hospital onboard?" Frank's whole world was spinning, but he pressed forward. "Like an infirmary? Somethin' more than a roll o' *gauze?* We been through some serious shit here — as you can tell. And food, please. My friend here's losin' it."

The stray Captains were quickly informed that the supply ship had a fully functional, and even *well-respected* restaurant onboard — something about diversifying their business in a tough space economy.

"So you're like — a big fuckin' ice cream truck? Huh."

Duncan nodded thoughtfully. "Runnin' on rocket fuel."

"Good one, Dunko. Hey, you — c'mere." Frank pointed shakily at one of their rescuers and lowered his voice to a whisper. "You got any — baked goods back there? Dessert shit?"

He was informed, politely but a little formally, that they offered *paying customers* a plentiful array of freshly baked delights. "Yeah — alright. Good." Frank threw up in his mouth, and valiantly swallowed it down again. "What're the specials? You got ham?"

Duncan took Frank's arm around his shoulder — once they'd excavated him from that medieval death trap — and helped him to a table. As luck would have it, Duncan's wallet had been found *intact* in his suit — and so they were finally, enthusiastically *welcomed aboard*. Sandwiches, snacks, appetizers and drinks — it was a bountiful feast.

"Hey, kid, you still hungry?"

"No way, Frank. I'm gonna explode."

Frank winced, remembering *The Apollo*. "That's alright, but — I gotta do somethin'." He snapped his fingers and winced again. The waiter began his long approach. "I remembered you, tellin' me about yer Dad. When you were a kid, every weekend — right? Well, I had them whip this up for ya." Frank's mouth tightened, and he squeezed one of Duncan's shoulders. "Anyway, thanks for comin' back for me."

Duncan smiled, and nodded back at Frank. He even didn't need to look up as the waiter arrived. He could already smell the citrus. "No Problem, Captain. Much obliged." And for the first time in a long time, Duncan Arugula leaned back in his chair, and felt truly at ease.

THE END

INTERVIEW WITH THE AUTHOR:
The Making of *Lemon Tarts in Space!*

In conversation with Maggie Fucile, co-host of the podcast *Second Breakfast with Cam & Maggie*

[This transcript has been edited for clarity]

Maggie: Let's talk about the origins of *Lemon Tarts*. I have the privilege of being married to you – so I know things, and I know you've been working on this for a long time. And what I mean by that is that you started working on it a long time ago, and then you returned to it again very recently. So when did you first start writing *Lemon Tarts*? And how did you get to where we are now?

Cam: So I was working on a horror book – that one's still kind of a work in progress, it's something I'm tinkering with, it will be the only thing that matters after my death. It's the *Faustus* book. I was spending many months in the *Faustus* trenches. And that was tough. It's horror, it's drama, it's religion, it's big ideas and tension. And I love all that – there's a melancholy and misery that I really take to in that headspace. The day after I finished that project, I just needed to get something else out of my system. I had been repressing all of the silly, dumb bullshit that I like doing in comedies for so long. It had been a few years since I'd written a comedy. So the day after I finished [the *Faustus*] project, I just cranked out this short story. It didn't even have a title - I think the document on my computer is still called "Untitled Science Fiction Project." And I basically wrote it in one go. It was around three-thousand words, and eventually I called it *Lemon Tarts*, just as a vernacular in my head. It was a one-off story about a space captain on this ship and he was being chased around by this little green blob of an alien. And I didn't know what to call [the alien], I didn't know if I was going to make up some proper noun for it - you know, like 'xenomorph'. But it was loosely, I mean, not intentionally - but after the fact I can definitely see that it was - inspired by the last act of *Alien*. And that whole cat-and-mouse rivalry, with the one human and the one alien - I love the tension there. But doing it in the silliest way possible, by having the character be really, *really* dumb and goofy and pretentious, and having the alien be this devouring, screeching, squealing monster - I just liked that. I like simple concepts, two characters going back and forth. So I did that in one day, and I had this little story, got it out of my system, and then I rebalanced and moved on to a hundred other projects. And then it was three or four years later -

M: I was going to say, I remember you wrote that first short story in 2020, because it was during the pandemic. And so then you went back to this about a year ago now, so that would have been a three-year gap.

C: Creatively, I sort of set aside 2024 to go back to unfinished projects, and I've got a lot of those. Some of them are like a couple yards from the finish line, some of them are just gestures. And I kind of interviewed myself - speed dating all of these different projects to see what was speaking to me now. And for some reason *Lemon Tarts* was, and that was weird, because I thought it was done. I thought that was just a little short story. But I had this idea for another story - I even did cover art for it, another sci-fi-tinged story with a very small cast and a really dark, wicked sense of humor. Because even though the character in that first chapter of *Lemon Tarts* is dumb, I think the humor's really sharp - it's not goofy and light, you know, it's really sharp and deadly – and that's what was speaking to me. So I had an idea for this other story called *Electric Tumor*, and it was basically making the alien a big tumor, to be able to talk about cancer and play with a bunch of these ideas, but in a physical form. Instead of just having it be "an invader from outer space in a far-off land," I wanted it to be something that felt more personal and tangible. So I was batting around that idea, and I realized it was almost a prequel to the *Lemon Tarts* idea, and then the gears started turning. Instead of having two connected short stories, it bubbled into three, and I thought, "What would happen if these characters met?", and "How can I blend these timelines?" – and then I bought a corkboard and I started putting up index cards of interesting scenes and chapter titles, and then it turned into six chapters that would go across this saga of these two space captains and this alien that's really a tumor. And in the writing of it, that then ballooned into ten full chapters. So I didn't expect any of this to turn into a project as big and thorough as it is, but it was so great to return to comedy so many years later, and I found the writing of this project incredibly liberating and freeing.

M: I imagine that the creative projects that are the most rewarding are the ones that unfold in ways you don't expect or ways that you hadn't planned on, and then they just become sentient on their own and have their own agency. I imagine that can be really fun for you as a creator.

C: Yeah – I mean it's agony most of the time, slamming your head against a wall and trying to solve problems.

M: I know, I've seen it!

C: But when it is working, and when it does fly out of your control – I mean it's Nicole Kidman, it's "that indescribable feeling as the lights begin to dim". It's that. And there were a lot of those moments here and I tried to let that breathe more than I usually would, I tried to dance around the outline instead of being how I normally would be on the podcast. Listeners will be familiar with this: Maggie comes in loose, and she has minimal notes, and she can dance around and respond to stuff; Tristan is like this too. And I have rigorous notes and structure and outlines. I'm not really like that in the creative space. There is a lot of problem solving and structure, but there is a lot more looseness there too. And I was really trying to lean into enjoying both of those halves of the process here, which is why I let this thing accordion out from being three-thousand words to *thirty*-something, however long it is.

M: That's interesting that you wanted to be so loose and organic with it when you've chosen a genre like sci-fi that's so much more restrictive. Comedy is open and fluid and responsive and spontaneous and improvisational - but I feel like sci-fi is rigid. What drew you to do something that was a little less familiar to you? Because you said you'd written a lot of comedy before, and you still continue to now - I feel like that's one of your biggest things - but sci-fi was new for you. So what drew you to do that?

C: I'm reminded of something Tristan told me about myself. You guys are both good for that. You tell me truths about myself that I would never see otherwise. And one of them was basically, every time I say something about myself or just make declarations about me and what I like and who I am, I'm usually wrong. Those are usually outdated things I just say without even questioning or believing them. And one of them is that I don't really like sci-fi. I think I've said this before, that I prefer to watch or play sci-fi, and I prefer to read fantasy. But I have *technically* worked in science fiction a little bit before: a similar story to this one, I started writing a short story about lobsters that was supposed to be two pages, and it turned into a sixty-thousand-word novel. I have to do a little editing, and then I'll get that one out into the universe too. But that one ended up with some sci-fi elements in it. But this is the first, you know, "captains, spaceships, the moon" sci-fi that I've ever really done.

And I think I learned to ignore what I used to view as the limitations of the genre. [*Lemon Tarts* is] sort of a grab bag of things I love within this genre, because it's not true that I don't like sci-fi. I love *Hitchhiker's Guide to the Galaxy*. I think if you're talking about comedy in sci-fi, that's the elephant in the room. But I don't think it's the only influence. I think it did scare me away from the genre for a while, because I'd felt like, "Oh, it has been done to perfection." But I think again, I'm wrong, because one of the series I grew up on – I mean, we talk about *Harry Potter* and millennials, and these things being baked into our DNA as incredibly strong cultural memories – but equally right on that level, for me, when I was growing up, was

Artemis Fowl, and that's sci fi too! It's not in space, so I never thought about it that way, but it's all about tech. It's absolutely sci fi. And I love that book so much as an adventure. We did an episode about the first *Star Wars* movie, which I still think is the best science fiction movie. It's such a fun, propulsive adventure. And I love how light the science is there. And then, of course, after I finished writing this, I got into *Dune*, but that's hard sci-fi, and that is not me [as a writer]. But the other things that I really loved and tried to kind of roll into the blender, the smoothie of whatever this project is, were some of the sci-fi stories I love to play, because as much as I grew up with *Artemis Fowl*, I grew up with *Halo* and *Gears of War*. And those are sci-fi too, right? Those are big, rollicking, almost explosive, blockbuster adventure stories. And I think when you walk through Barnes & Noble and you see sci-fi, and it's all of these dour covers and boring fonts and the books are all a million pages – I think that's why I had this idea in my head that I didn't like sci-fi. But I love so many of these elements across *this* medium or *that* medium, and rolling them all into one and just doing what I liked about sci-fi, instead of having to obey a genre convention – this project was me discovering, or maybe remembering, how much I love science fiction.

M: You described [*Lemon Tarts*] as "light sci-fi". Apart from the comedy that gives the whole thing an element of levity, what else feels "light sci-fi" about it to you? Like, what distinguishes it from, you know, a "homework book"?

C: One of the rules – every creative project I do, I put rules on it, and I think those help me just learn, and it gives you a small box to play in. I think we've talked about this with Jack White – the more creative restrictions you put on yourself, the more you have to be creative to find solutions. Sometimes you have to put those shackles on yourself to give you something to strain against or react to. That lobster book, for example, is a comedy without dialogue. I wanted to see if I could make a comedy funny without verbal sparring and punchlines. So I did a lot of creative limitations for [*Lemon Tarts*] too. And one of those, because I was working in sci-fi (and I don't like that dry, hard sci-fi thing – I mean, I do now because of *Dune*, but you know what I mean, right?) –

M: That's not what you wanted to focus on.

C: Right, I would never write like Frank Herbert, that's just not my thing. So one of the rules I put on myself for this project was absolutely zero research, which I think makes it the most *lightweight* science fiction book you will ever read. And a lot of that - I gotta shout out my sister here, we affectionately call her "Brother Sameron" on the podcast, but of course, she's my twin sister Sam - and she's always complimented my stupidity. I realized I couldn't do a better sci-fi comedy than *Artemis Fowl* or *Hitchhiker*. Those are the mountaintop, I'm not going to be on Mount Rushmore with Douglas Adams and Eoin Colfer. I'm not, and that's fine. I can worship them from down here, I'm happy with that. But I realized that even if I can't make a 'better' sci-fi comedy than them, *sure as shit, I can make a dumber one.* And the thing Sam has always loved from me is the dumb stuff. Just like riffing and making up fake histories when I don't know anything about a subject, just kind of worming my way to a solution. There was a moment in the Cheesecake Factory where I was trying to describe different eras of history - anyway. There's a dumbness built into this story because I couldn't look up how anything about space travel worked, or anything about the 1960s or NASA or the Cold War, or the Bay of Pigs - all of these subjects become monologues in the book, with the narrator trying to bullshit their way towards an explanation and trying to figure it out with context clues. Leaning into the stupid and really having fun there, and not taking the science part of science fiction too seriously – like homework, like you said – I think that's what makes this light, and what makes it funny, instead of trying to intellectualize it and going for something that's *clever*. I think this is much funnier.

M: Well, I feel like that makes it more accessible, too. I think a lot of people don't feel like classic sci-fi is for them, because it feels intimidating, or it feels like – if I find something that's hard sci-fi, I kind of feel a little stupid when I read it, because I'm like, "Oh, I don't really understand how this technology works, or this scientific phenomenon that they're discussing." Reading your book, it made me feel smart, because I was like, "Well, I don't know a lot about space travel, but, you know what? I also kind of don't know what the Bay of Pigs was either – I don't think it was actual pigs, but I don't really know." And so it makes you feel like, "Okay, we're in a safe space. We can have stupid thoughts." Like, I know that a hairdryer is not going to be an effective weapon against an alien, but I like that it is in this story. You're on this interesting level of absurdity where anything is possible, which is what's fun about sci-fi off the bat; there's all this creative freedom, like anything is possible because you're going beyond the limitations of our current technological situation. So that absurdity makes it just fun and playful.

C: It should be wondrous and creative. That's why we talk about how predictive science fiction can be. You see *Star Trek* having touchscreen smartphones like forty years before we did. And I think you can turn that in a comedic direction and just have fun with it. There's a plot point in the book that is about *Apollo 11*, and that means that I needed to figure out, "Why did we have to get to number eleven? What happened with the first ten?" And I know, I guess, in my head that they all had different problems, but coming up with a comedic bit for each one of those previous *Apollo* missions, that's fun and stupid. I can make that as dumb as humanly possible and have fun with that. So yeah, I think that's where I tried to look into my total ignorance as a comedic opportunity.

M: I like that, because then you have the two genres working together and not fighting against one another. Can you tell me more about any other creative limitations or rules that you put on this project? I know that you do that for all of your projects. There's always some sort of word count rule or a limit about how the structure of the chapters should work. What were some of those creative limitations that you added to this book?

C: The first one that pops into my mind is this idea of duality. I really like two-word titles. I really like two-character stories, these two handers. We talk about *Doctor Faustus* or *Frankenstein* or a modern example, like *The Lighthouse*. I just like these stories. So this story basically has two characters, every title of every chapter is two words or a contraction, and almost every line, almost every joke, almost every metaphor or image, and all the important lines of dialogue – this was part of the outlining and the structure – they all come back. There is this idea of repetition and reframing. And I like that sort of couplet idea of bringing something back in a different context. It's not just a callback, but it has a different resonance and feel to it. So there is an incredible level of duality baked into this, if you're looking for it. If not, maybe some of them will click for you, but that was fun for me to structure it in a call-and-response sort of way.

M: Yeah, that sounds really fun. And without spoiling anything, I think that helps us understand why your final chapter is called "Echo Chamber" – this idea of things coming back, and that's really lovely.

C: Two captains, two ships, two timelines – yeah, it's a good rule.

M: Did you have word count limitations for your chapters? Or how you wanted each chapter to wrap up?

C: This one was looser than some of the other ones I've done. It was loosely three-thousand words. Again, I went in with the corkboard: I had six chapters outlined, and I tried to have fun. You want to dance around the outline, you don't want a character decision to feel like a plot point that's just happening. You want them to grapple with it, you want them to consider the other options. So in execution, it will always take a little longer than you're expecting. So I tried to be looser with that, which meant opening up the word count a little bit. It was roughly three-thousand words, but it went more or less depending. And in the audio drama version, which is sort of the one that's a little closer to my heart – all of them average right around twenty minutes as episodes, which also leans into kind of a sitcom feel. It gives it, I think, more of that comedic structure that we're used to. John Cleese talked about a movie being a really tough venue for comedy, because you really want to be short and sweet. You don't want to overstay your welcome. You don't want people to get sick of the characters, the archetypes, the jokes. You want to just get in and out. And viewing this in an episodic way – I mean, it turned out to be ten episodes or chapters – I was viewing those as individual pieces. I mean, we talk about comics a lot on the podcast, and I was trying to structure this in a way of, "If this were like a ten-issue miniseries, and you picked up one of them and you read through it, would you feel satisfied? Would you feel like you got your money's worth?" You got a few laughs, you got some plot movement…And I think that sort of balancing made sure I didn't have one clear favorite chapter. I didn't want one to be, "Oh, this is where all the funny stuff happens, this is the plot one, and these three are set-up."

We talked about this a lot on the *House of the Dragon* episodes with Tristan. And I think one of the points we made there was that set-up doesn't have to be boring. It doesn't have to *feel* like set-up. There's a magic trick when you're telling a story where you can be setting up fifty different things at the same time, and the audience doesn't realize it. You can have an adventure that sets up something else quietly in the background. So I didn't want to have any downtime. I wanted to have this episodic, exciting structure, but that was one of the rules: no downtime chapters, everything has to circle back, and make it feel worthwhile and episodic, like those chunks you remember from the first *Star Wars*, those scenes that really stick with you, those levels that I love so much from *Halo* or *Gears of War*. Try to evoke the best parts of the genre. Do it quick, be punchy, and then get the fuck out of there.

M: And I think, apart from the final chapter, they all end on a cliffhanger, right? So again, it's adding to that level of excitement, because I think that's also what you seem to be leaning into in the sci-fi thing – not just the silliness and the technology and the creativity, but also how adventurous and exciting it can be, leaning into that *Alien* thing you talked about.

C: I take that back to the Adam West *Batman*, ending on the cliffhanger of 'same bat time, same bat channel,' I always find that exciting and worthwhile. So if you can end with a knockout character revelation or a nail-biting cliffhanger, do that as much as humanly possible. I mean, if the first chapter is the last chunk of *Alien*, it's a very silly version of a slasher, with a really overpowered alien and a really dumb final boy. So if you can keep some of that going, you've got some of that built in suspense and cliffhangers and cat and mouse kind of reversals. I really wanted to just pedal-to-the-metal this. It could have been longer – I wanted it to be as tight as possible. You know, you cut the jokes that aren't quite up to snuff. You cut the side plots – I want this to be all killer no filler.

M: I really think it is. You went beyond what your original limitation was. You'd planned for six chapters, and you let it organically grow into ten, but I still think even with that, it's very tight and neat. Can you tell me more about your process? Just being married to you, seeing you create things for the last ten to fifteen years, I know that you have different processes for each thing that you create. And I mean that in terms of influences that you're engaging with, like you talked about John Cleese and Douglas Adams and Eoin Colfer, but

I know that you've always got a specific playlist for whatever project you're working on, or you exclusively write on a typewriter, or you exclusively write on your computer or by hand. Tell me about what the actual writing process was like before you moved into any of the audio production and all of that.

C: I've got a couple things that just came to mind. One is that I wrote most of this by hand in libraries. When I was working on the *Faustus* project, I wrote that by hand in little notebooks in churches around New York almost every day. And I found that to be just an incredible experience, it really changed the way you felt. So I tried to do some of that here. And when I was typing into the computer, or I got in a groove and I was writing on the computer, my entire draft was in Courier New, which is that old-timey typewriter font, and that is the feel of the sci-fi I like. We were talking about *Alien: Romulus* a few weeks ago – I loved that movie because it leaned into the aesthetic of the original, and the aesthetic of *Alien* is as good as the alien. You know, you want the big buttons. You want the blinking lights. I love that so much in *Star Wars* – anytime you have a wall of blinking lights, that's fucking sci-fi.

M: Yeah, all the buttons, all the clicky, clacky - I don't know what any of these buttons do, but I'm so excited about them!

C: Yeah, computers talking, it's kind of scary. All the lights in *2001: A Space Odyssey* - that stuff is what I gravitate to. Actually, when I wrote the short story version years ago, it was in Microsoft Word at the time: I made the background black and I made the font bright green, because that's what I wanted it to be! That's what I want sci-fi to feel like. The glory of self-publishing - and you were talking about me wearing a lot of hats - is that I can make those decisions. And when I made the decision to publish this book in Courier New, I think that's sort of an olive branch of, "This is what I love about sci-fi. Take my hand, join me on this journey, and let's go have fun with it," instead of, "Well, it has to be in a respectable Garamond or Cambria," or all these stupid-ass, official, respectable *New York Times* best-seller fonts. You know, fuck that. I wanted this to be fun. It's supposed to be funny. And I think this font - I mean, this sounds stupid, but when you're staring at a screen all day, when you're in your head coming up with ideas - Courier New is a funnier font. It's goofier. So that's my answer, I guess, for how I got myself in the mood there. And musically, this one was weird. You're right that I always have a playlist. And it's never music that's tonally appropriate.

M: That's what's so interesting about it. It's never like, "Oh well, I'm gonna listen to the *Alien* soundtrack," it's never anything like that. For this one I remember you listening to Nine Inch Nails.

C: Yeah, it's never what you expect. But I always write to music. I always have music going, and I'll end up just looping something, whether it's an artist or an album. Sometimes it's a song, I've spent five hours writing to the same song before. If you find that groove, you've just got to hold on to it as tight as you can. There were a couple big musical influences here. A lot of it was the harder, earlier, Nine Inch Nails stuff, and some of those remixes. I think that industrial metal sound has some of that sci-fi aesthetic that I like to it. I just said it was discordant, but I think there is some of that there, because if you were to describe the aesthetic of *Alien*, I think you would mention it feeling industrial – Weyland Yutani. And the thing we love about *Star Wars* is all of the ships that have this brushed, screwed up old metal, or when you're in the Empire ships, and it's all this strict

white or strict black…there is an industrial
feeling to a lot of these aesthetics. And I
like to kind of ride the wave of music. And no
one creates better waves or vibes than Trent
Reznor in Nine Inch Nails.

I also - I mean, we'll talk about this in a
bit, I'm sure - but a lot of this book is
wrapped up in me and Tristan. And he, of course,
is one of our lead characters in the audio
drama version as Captain Duncan Arugula. And I
remember, this was about 10 years ago now,
because we're all getting obscenely old, that
he turned us onto a band called Royal Blood.
Which, back to the duality thing, is a two-
piece. I love two-piece bands more than
anything else: The Kills, The White Stripes.
And Royal Blood, it's just bass and drums. And
they hit like a freight train. The bass tone
that he gets is just sick, and the drums are
just pounding on your chest. Those first couple
albums are so good, and then they went in this
weird, almost dance, a little bit of techno-y
direction. And those albums never made sense
to me. And I always go back to albums from
artists I love that I don't get, to try to make
sense of them. And I was just in that groove
here. And some of those newer songs clicked for
me, some of those more dance-y songs, they
clicked for me while I was starting this

project. The song "Oblivion," off of their third album, *Typhoons*, I listened to that probably a thousand times while writing this book. And then for the quieter moments, because a book can't just be one tone, or you would grow numb to it - especially when you're playing with cancer and a slasher and all sorts of fun shit - you need some character moments that are quieter, you need some contemplation, some reflection, some grief, whatever the scene calls for. So I went back to a lot of early delta blues. So the playlist - if you shuffle it, which is what I do - is chaos. It's an absolute mess. But I think those three things together helped me kind of ride the lightning toward this strange, negotiated tone that the project demanded.

M: I really like that. I wonder if we should make those playlists public.

C: If you know how to do that, then I'll do that.
M: Okay, that'll be fun! Little perk - really get in tune with Cam's psyche," I guess. No, I love that.

C: I wish you all could see how wide Maggie's eyes just went.

M: I just got so excited.

C: *Laughs.* "Psyche." How polite.

M: It's just…it's wild in there. Can you tell us more about the format? This is an audio drama, but it's also a novel. And you've got this history with audio drama – that was really, I think, your first love, and the first things that you wrote and did with Tristan were proper audio dramas. They weren't even available as text. And in other projects you've done, you've made the scripts available to read. But in this project, you've got the full audio drama, but you've also got a novelization that goes beyond just the pure script of the audio drama. So can you talk about 1) why you made the choice to have both of those formats? And 2) how the adaptation of the novel form affected the final project? What was that like?

C: There's a lot there, so you'll have to help me if I get too off track. I say this to people all the time, because we do the podcast two or three times a week: I believe in audio. We're available on YouTube too, but I view [*Second Breakfast with Cam & Maggie*] as a podcast. I genuinely really love the auditory medium, whether it is audiobooks or podcasts or music, like we just spent ten minutes on. I believe in audio. I don't think it is a little sibling to video. I don't think video podcasts are better than audio podcasts. If anything, I think focusing on that one element is everything. So as a storyteller, I think audio dramas are sort of the perfect form, because a lot of storytelling is engaging someone's imagination, right? Even if they're watching the same movie or reading the same book, everyone's going to come away with a different version of it, a different impression, a different feeling, almost a different experience, which is fascinating. And you can't write for all of that, but I think that's a fun side effect of it.

M: I think that's why I like reading books so much, because it's so personal and subjective.

C: I feel like books give you the most room to participate, to put your own stink on whatever line of dialogue you're reading to interpret things in different ways. That's why we can debate Shakespeare or Marlowe four-hundred years later. Because you can read *King Lear*, you can read *Othello* a million different ways, and they're all equal. That's part of what I love to do [on the podcast] when we're spitting dumb theories about works of art. I think that's where that comes from. But in the audio field, you also get some performance. And this is where, because I'm a control freak - I mean, when I give someone a gift, I let them unwrap it, and then I take it back from them and explain it to them and tell them why they should like it -

M: It's quite an experience to receive a gift from Cam, and it's always the most thoughtful gift you've ever received - so it's worth it to let you take it right back and tell me all about it.

C: But that part's important to me, too. And if you're writing a novel or you're writing a short story, you have complete control. And I think that can be as good as it can be bad. So in a form like audio drama, or even a straight audiobook - like I told you, the book about lobsters, no dialogue there, that's just narration. That is more of a straightforward audiobook, but there's still performance there. There are still jokes that you're telling, and performances. I remember when I was in college, when I found the audio drama format - because I'd been listening to MuggleCast since I was 14, on an iPod Nano while emptying out my dog's litter box - I distinctly remember that experience, I don't know why! Some things, the needle just drops, and you lock in those memories. But when I discovered the audio drama format, I think it was as important to me as the substance of *Hitchhiker's Guide to the Galaxy*, because it felt like the perfect happy medium of all of these different things I loved, because I loved that performance aspect. When I was in college, I bought a cassette tape on eBay of an audiobook of the first *Hitchhiker* book that Douglas Adams read himself, *because I enjoy author's intent*. I enjoy the way an author felt about a book. Imagine if we had Charles Dickens reading some of his stories. Imagine if we had Shakespeare perform – because he did perform as well – imagine if you had him performing "To be or not to be", and you could see, like, "What is the canon way to enunciate in that speech?"

M: "What did he intend? What was his actual vision?" Yeah, that would feel like the purest form of that text.

C: I'm of two minds here, because I love an amazing audiobook, or audio drama performance from a professional actor. They can bring it to life. Like *Hard Times* by Charles Dickens – the guy who played the freaky Maester who brought the Mountain back to life in *Game of Thrones*, Qyburn – that actor's name is Anton Lesser, and he did an audiobook of *Hard Times* by Charles Dickens, which I read in grad school. And he brought that story to life in a way that - me reading the book - I would never have understood it that well. He had an intimacy, a familiarity. He breathed life into that text in an almost miraculous way. Dan Stevens doing *Frankenstein*, same thing. So on one hand, I really love when a great actor can add their own spin to a book and really take it to the next level. But I also love that idea of an author reading their own story, and that inflection and that feeling - I think they're both valuable. So when I discovered that I could sort of split the difference there, and perform my stories, but also be the author? Because, especially when you're writing comedy - I hear the punchlines in my head, I know the voice of the character, and I know how they're delivering or putting a spin on a certain line - if I can live up to that, if I can be as good an actor as I am in my head (which I think is the torture of all authors), if you can live up to that vision, whatever that fleeting runaway thing in your head is - that's the dream.

And I think the audio drama is the only format that can really bottle that experience. Because if you're making a movie, there are a million other people, millions of dollars, studios, all sorts of interference separating you from a pure artistic vision. Sometimes writer/directors will get close, but you're still telling someone what to think and what to see, and that's fine, but I don't think that's where my 'author heart' lives. So if I'm just making an audio drama, there's still space for you to picture however the fuck you want Captain Duncan Arugula to look. And I never ever describe characters, because I don't care about that. I will give you their voices, and you can fill in the rest. I want to leave space for you as an audience member, as a reader, as a listener. I just want to do some of that work. I want to give you their voices. I want to tell you how the narration should be delivered, and then let you run away with the rest of it. And I think the audio drama is the perfect format for that. It's incredibly difficult, because I can second guess it to death. I can re-record it to death, because it has to live up to this fucking platonic ideal that's haunting and torturing me in my head. But when you do it, and when you have the discipline to try to get there, I think that is the closest I can get to handing you part of my brain, and that's what a book is.

M: I love that. And so then when you've got this novel version, you can no longer rely on the performances of you and Tristan carrying the interpretation of the book, carrying that feeling. And so that was sort of your challenge. I remember when you said, "Well, I want to have this as a novel as well, but if you just have the script, you can't have the inflection that I put on a joke. You can't have the voice crack that Duncan has when he's terrified." So then you had the challenge of putting it into a novel version to still give the audience some of those cues and help demonstrate your vision. But I know it was hard for you, and it was different than just having a script. So can you talk about that process?

C: It was an incredible challenge. And I mean that in a good way. I think that helped me grow and learn a lot from that experience. But when you start it, you don't want to just sub in stage direction. You don't want to just throw in tonal cues or adverbs every time someone opens their mouth. You don't want to over explain things and remove all that interpretation. There's a rhythm to storytelling, and to comedy. So the more you explain, you slow it down, you ruin that flow. And there are also things in audio that you can't translate. There are sound effects in this book that I made – I made all of them with my mouth, I don't use other things. If I want a door closing, if there's a moment where someone is talking over an intercom and they turn off the radio, I make that sound. I think that's fun, and it's also funnier, the more lo-fi and simple that is. But how do you turn that into a line in a novel? Even if you do over explain it, it's not funny anymore. So I had to find a lot of these moments where I could accent a feeling. I would listen back to a chapter from the audio drama and then try to shift it and convert this script into a novel. And that is when I moved past the idea of, "okay, we're just doing stage direction for all of this shit" into "this is an opportunity for me to get more jokes in there". You can explain how a character is feeling, you can say that they're on the verge of crying, or there's a voice crack, but there's a funny way to do that. You turn this into a creative challenge instead of just a logistical challenge. And at this point, they are two different beasts.

I feel like being in the shoes of this project helped me understand Douglas Adams a little more. He's still the mountaintop and I'm on the ground level, but the way he wrote *Hitchhiker's Guide to the Galaxy* as an audio drama, and then he adapted it, years later, into a novel, and then he wrote the screenplay for the movie. So those are all different beasts. There are different lines, characters feel different. And

I always struggled with that in the early days of like, "Which one is canon? Which one is my favorite?" But having done something lesser but similar now, they're different beasts. I will always feel fonder of the audio drama, because there's so much of me in that, there's so much of Tristan in that, and us playing around together and doing these voices and the sound effects and the noises that the alien makes. I mean, in the script, there is stage direction for that, so when I record, I know what kind of sneezing, squirtling snarl to make, like I know how to do that. But the novel is its own beast now, and it has a couple hundred jokes or changes that aren't in the audio drama, and being okay with that has made me feel very happy about having this as a novel. I know some people don't like audio. I know some people can't really process audio books. Obviously, some people can't hear as well. So I wanted to have it available in different formats here, and I think they are distinct but interesting beasts. I didn't want it to feel like just publishing a script. I think this is a novel. This is not a tweaked screenplay or something. It is a novel.

M: No, you're so right. I was going to say that I've listened to and read both versions, and they are distinct experiences, and both reward

you in unique ways. And I found it very valuable
and rewarding and fun to experience both. And
I like that it means it appeals to more kinds
of people, more readers, more enjoyers of
stories.

C: And I know as myself, because I am a control
freak and I like to really hyper fixate on
things I love, I really enjoy reading all the
different versions of *Hitchhiker*, and kind of
parsing the differences. So if anyone were to
care about this story enough, I think there is
some meat on the bone there. There are some
different things you'll notice in one medium
versus the next.

M: Earlier, you alluded to this, but I want to
talk about it more. You talked about when you
wrote "Electric Tumor", the second short story
that became basically the second chapter of
[*Lemon Tarts*]. Obviously, there's a connection
to cancer. And I know that asking an author
about their personal experience can sometimes
be so dull or induce a lot of eye rolling,
because artists are not always drawing on their
own exclusive personal experience in their own
work. Sometimes you're just writing about a
subject because it's interesting, not because
it's your own personal experience. But I happen
to know that there is a clear personal

connection in *Lemon Tarts* with the cancer allegory. So I would love if you could talk about that, and what parts of the cancer or cancer-adjacent experience were important for you to include and explore in this book.

C: So I've talked about this at some length before. I did an episode [of the podcast] about *Fallout 3*, and I talked about cancer a lot in that one. That was probably the most personal I've gotten about this. But I guess the TL;DR here is just that I have a lot of experience with cancer, and years and years and years of my mom having breast cancer and ultimately dying from that through my childhood and adolescence. And obviously that was the most formative thing that has ever happened in my life, from the time I was fourteen to just about twenty-one. She had the most aggressive form of breast cancer possible, and fought like a bat out of hell for that many years through chemo, radiation, surgery and clinical trials. I've seen as ugly as this can get. And it's not just that, it's as many grandparents as you can name, and dogs and all through the family tree, there's cancer there. So that has influenced, I think, a lot of the things I've made in different ways. The *Faustus* book, when that's eventually out there, there's a lot of grief in that book. And that's horror, which I think plays with grief in a different way. [*Lemon Tarts*] is not about grief. This is a comedy. And I think grief is almost overdone in the last 10 years.

M: Yeah, the *Hereditary* train really set it in motion.

C: And I think it's been done incredibly well – *The Haunting of Hill House*, like you said, *Hereditary*, *The Babadook*. I think a lot of those stories are gorgeous, but I don't have anything to add there. I wanted to talk about cancer in a way that was interesting and challenging. This book is not about me, it's not about my experience, it's not about my family. It is a jumping off point. I think there are experiences and feelings and part of the world and human condition you see when you go through that forever, and move around the country and go to different hospitals. There's a feeling of impotence and powerlessness and resentment, and it takes you in sort of a philosophical, existential direction. And the thing I love about sci-fi – I was cheering at the screen watching *Alien: Romulus* every time there was a beautiful, sad, melancholy shot of a spaceship floating through space with this incredible, massive planet or asteroid belt in the background – I find that genre contemplative, and I found myself diving deeper and deeper into that. And, this is the most fun part, turning it into comedy. I wrote and published my first book a month after my mom died, and wrote the majority of that book – which was the most balls-to-the-wall, just punchlines, just be as funny as humanly possible – I wrote the majority of that book while she was in hospice at home. So I have always had the link of comedy and the most traumatic, fucked up, imaginable things happening. I've always linked those things, and I think it makes me funnier. I think it sort of breaks down the inhibitions a little bit. There's something liberating about seeing the worst possible things that can happen. So I wanted to talk about cancer in a way that I found challenging, instead of just "cancer bad". What if you make cancer the alien, and then that alien is kind of a character. I guess minor spoilers here, but one of those aliens who, in this story, I call the Problem, one of these Problems becomes more of a character through the course of the book. We give him a name and we follow him. So the idea of getting inside cancer's head and writing it as a character, in a comedy – a very violent, dark comedy – that is a fun creative challenge for me. That is not me writing my "sad memoir." That is something fun and worthwhile from a comedic perspective. So that's how I tried to kind of spin it into something that was rewarding, instead of just navel gazing.

M: Did you find that in doing this, did it help you work through any of these things? I mean, none of this is fresh, it's been in your life for a long time, and your mom died almost ten years ago. But did you find that you better understood something about yourself, or your experience, or anything like that? Was it a therapeutic exercise in any way? Or was it more just an interesting springboard for a creative experience?

C: I think I made it funnier. I think I've always enjoyed cancer jokes. We talked about this in an episode about *Deadpool* over on Patreon - that trilogy, talking about the movements and vacillations between those three movies. And I've always talked about the first *Deadpool* as being my favorite cancer movie because it is the funniest and freest with that subject matter. I mean, there are plenty of cancer movies that take it on its face and they're incredibly moving and worthwhile. In the same way that there are movies about grief and all these other heavy subjects. *A Monster Calls*, that's another cancer movie that takes it plain faced. It has some fantastical, surreal elements, but it's a straightforward negotiation of that topic. But I love how rough *Deadpool* is with the cancer comedy, and I find a lot of release in that. I think going to a sad cancer movie and going to a funny one, they are cathartic in different ways. So I think I make some of some really good cancer jokes in there, and I earned those fucking things, and I stand by [the idea] that humor is the only way to get through bad shit. I think it brings people together, it takes power away from the bad thing, and it makes you laugh without you choosing to. It's involuntary. It's dark. This is why I call it a dark comedy. I mean, when I call it light science fiction, dark comedy, I'm saying "dark" as a polite way to say cancer. It's a light science fiction sci-fi cancer comedy. That's what this is. So I don't think it was about helping me work through anything. I really, really liked the challenge of writing a character who was this writhing, gnashing, monstrous blob. I mean, he's basically, "What if Flubber was a tumor?" That's what the Problem is. And I think I learned from that, and I learned from having to decide where that character goes and what that character wants. I think I have a bit of a fuller understanding. But that was never the objective.

M: But again, it's nice that it just organically unfolded, and that became what the process was and what the experience was for you.

C: Yeah, there are characters in the book who have had cancer and have a closer relationship with the tumor and these subjects, and getting inside their heads and finding the comedy there was interesting. But this was not never meant to be therapeutic for me, it was meant to be as funny as humanly possible.

M: It seems like, much in the way all of your creative stuff is, it just becomes therapeutic for you in that it's the thing that you love.

C: The way to honor this subject matter is not to be saccharine or to make it "Important". I think it's to make it the funniest book that I wish my mom could read as one of the funniest people I've ever met, I think that was my objective.

M: I like that. I think, I mean, I *know* your mom would have loved this book. She would have cracked up. I know that you intentionally included the cancer thing, and that was a thoughtful, thought-out thing that you included in this book. But in a lot of your projects, I notice that a lot of your other personal things end up in there, with or without your intention. Can you talk about other personal connections that are laced throughout *Lemon Tarts*?

C: There's a lot of dumb shit in there, I think sometimes the more specific you get, the more universally it connects with people. There's a reference in the book at one point to brownie on a stick, and that is something I used to get at our local bakery when I was a kid, and it just came to me in the moment, and I liked it. Or, you know, I have a beard, and having a beard means I have a fucking topiary strapped to my head that I have to tend to as a little garden every single day of my life. I have to groom and shape this thing. And there's a plot point about hairdryers being turned into weapons to fight the cancer alien. Like you're so far out on the branch there with stupid shit that it makes me smirk, the more dumb stuff you can involve there. There are jokes about oatmeal, because I started eating oatmeal. Like at some point you just surrender and let some of your life seep into the book. But it's those elements of me that I included, more than this being a cancer confessional. It's more about some stuff in my head, some isolation, some covid. The life of an author and a creative and a control freak is a lot of me staring at a brick fucking wall trying to solve a problem that no one else would even understand, never mind be able to settle. And there is a lot of loneliness there. And these two characters are two space captains in the middle of nowhere in different timelines who have been alone for a long time. So I think whether it's confidence or panic or a bunch of these other things that these guys go through - yeah, sure, I'll crib some of that from my own life.

M: That makes total sense. And I think a lot of these things from you end up being not necessarily intentional, or just kind of happenstance as part of the creative process. But I think it ends up giving the whole book just a really personal flavor. It feels very unique to you, but also, like you said, makes it easier to connect with as a reader, as a listener. Because it feels like, "Oh, a real person wrote this, and I can connect to it, even though maybe I've never had a brownie on a stick, but that seems like such a personal thing, and I also have personal memories of x, y and z." So rather than it being just super general, like any AI computer could write, but it's that an actual human being has touched this and has their own personal experiences laced throughout that also can be more generalized, and I can connect to in my own way.

C: Yeah, I think the other thing there is depictions of men. We talk about depictions of men a lot, and I think there's an element of men where there's a reluctance to be vulnerable, and maybe a difficulty with expressing emotions, in a coherent, self-aware way. There's a difficulty with that. And with the main two characters in this book both being men, I tried to work in some of that and explore masculinity. Not in the way that, I think, again, has just been done a lot in the past ten years, as a critique, as a takedown, as a deconstruction – that's all fine, but that's not what I'm interested in. I think exploring all the shades of masculinity, and how these two guys are going to interact and maybe compete and maybe lean on each other and learn from each other. And so much of that relationship is going to be unspoken, because that's how men communicate. Leaning into that implication, land how you can find that subtext in a performance. Or then, "Shit, I have to do a novel version. How do I write in those little pinpricks, those provocations to get you to go on that journey and read between the lines of the dialogue?" I had fun with that. But the other thing you're asking about things, I pulled from my own life here: this book is also, I think, a lot about Tristan and I. Because it's about male friendship, and he is my best friend and has been forever. And as two men – and you throw these two guys in the audio drama, so we are the main characters – I think there's a lot of that rolled in here too, and reflections and references and easter eggs and meditations, and I enjoyed those as jumping off points for comedy and drama.

M: And I think that as a listener, even if you don't know that the two of you are good friends, I think the personal history that you have with one another plays out in the book itself, because you both know so much about each other. And it's coming through in both of your performances.

C: Most of the audio dramas I've ever done, I've done with Tristan. I know how to write to his voice, I know how to write to his strengths, and then he will still come in and do things I never imagined. When I was talking about trying to be funny in the way that I am in person, when I was talking about my sister, and those kind of conversational stupidities that really make people giggle – I am at my funniest with Tristan. I am at my funniest around Tristan. And trying to capture some of that in the writing process is one thing, but then when you're bringing it to life, and you're in a room and you're holding the mics, and you've got to be funny on that level, bouncing off someone you trust and know, and then when that relationship is baked into the text? That was a fairly unbelievable experience.

M: Thank you so much for joining us today for this interview about *Lemon Tarts*. I'm so excited for you to launch this book.

C: Thank you very much!

www.ingramcontent.com/pod-product-compliance
Lightning Source LLC
Chambersburg PA
CBHW020109310726

48970CB00002B/556